FLOWERS FOR ALBATROSS

Published in Canada by Engen Books, St. John's, NL.

ISBN-13: 978-1-77478-005-3

Distributed by:
Engen Books
www.engenbooks.com
submissions@engenbooks.com

First mass market paperback printing: January 2021

Cover Design: Mandi Coates

Slipstreamers Committee:
Amanda Labonté
Ali House
AJ Ryan
Ellen Curtis
Erin Vance
Lauralana Dunne
Matthew LeDrew

FLOWERS FOR ALBATROSS

MATTHEW DANIELS & JD RYOT

CHAPTER ONE

Sky, horizon, treetops.

In that order.

There was a lurch as the plane went over the edge. It was a Cessna 140, fourth or fifth-hand. Old, well-maintained, sturdy, cheap. Cassidy had some bush piloting in her background. It was about the same as swimming: up good, down bad, and don't let your gas run out. Here she was, though, coming out of a hole in the sky and facing oh so much down. She was laughing.

Just as the engine began to build, she'd had people in the cave in her world push her out of the hole in the sky in the other world.

Most of the strapping of her outfit was for the pouches and tools she brought for her adventures. There was the seat belt, for what it was worth. The canopy filled her whole vision now that she was nosediving. Even so, at this height there should be a break in it. She'd seen mountains in the distance, before all that green. She could even smell it. Not a pine green. More lush.

Wind.

Everything leaned behind her. Behind was up. This

kind of freefall wasn't a zero-G experience. There were plenty of G's, and they were in a mad dash for the ground. She thrived in the adrenaline, even as part of her ran through possible maintenance oversights.

Hey, there are fruits above the canopy. Reddish-orange? How about that.

Eyes on the prize, guys. Time for the engine to do its thing. ...Now would be great.

Sputter.

Okay, okay. She's got this.

"Up and at 'em!" she shouted. She kicked hard at the floor and under the dash while she cursed, and her hands danced with the controls for the flaps and slats of the wings.

Eureka!

She wasn't sure if it was the wind or just this particular Cessna, but the engine roaring completely to life reminded her almost of the metallic teething of a chainsaw. Except the sound had been recorded and sped up, like a person speaking after inhaling helium.

Now the plane was adding even more acceleration to its nose-versus-ground race.

She pulled up so hard she felt it in her molars.

The sky was an earthquake. As the plane rattled like bushes in the wind, she righted her view so that now she could again see far and wide. "Ha! And they wanted me to take a pilot," Cassidy laughed at the clouds. "Can you imagine...?"

She banked. She didn't have to, but it felt great. Banking a plane was like surfing, just with a fuel tank and much higher stakes. Now she was parallel with the canopy, which was the closest thing to ground she could see until she made most of a circle in order to face roughly the direction she'd come from. Just how much she'd descended really struck home as she had to lean forward over the dash and crane her neck up to see the horizontal, ovaloid hole in the sky. From here, she couldn't see any of the people or equipment in the dig site on the other side of the portal. Just earthy red-brown in a vault of blue.

But then, it was much smaller from down here. Directly below the portal, a bizarre mountain stood at something like three or four thousand feet. It looked like a fault-block mountain, but also a fortress. If she could have seen through the front of the plane on her way down, she'd have noticed it then.

It was a ruined fortress. And to see it below the portal, it almost looked like it had coughed up the hole in the sky. Or maybe the rock had leaked down. She'd have to get closer to—

One of the "fruits" flew by her left wing and made a sound like a scream travelling through a tube!

"Whoa!" Cassidy spat out as she tilted the plane. More of the surreal shrieks sounded from different places. With the wind and the noise of the engine, she couldn't make out how many or where they were. "Let's drag, then!" she shouted. "Show me what you can do, baby," she said to the dashboard.

She went full throttle.

"Ha!" she cried out as some of the shrieks sounded farther away. But there was a metallic squeal and an organic, cawing shriek of primal rage above her. Unable to help herself, she looked up, but could see nothing from inside.

It was like the canopy was a carnival, letting up a flotilla of balloons which, now that she was getting a better look, were not fruit. Going faster didn't help when they were making a collision course. Other than blurs of black, blue, and brown, though, it was hard to get more than the sounds they made. She did her best duck-and-weave flying and shouted over her shoulder, "Take that!"

She thought she was winning.

The mountain was closer. It was like an empty set of torso armour standing out of the forest. If she didn't know any better, she'd have sworn that the material for the walls had come from the heights of the mountain. If that was true, though a ruin now…

One of the screaming things slap-landed full-body over the windows of the cockpit. Cassidy couldn't see the eyes because she was looking up at the underside of the neck and jaw. But the beak, comically short legs, and fanned-out membrane left no room for doubt:

It was a pterodactyl!

CHAPTER TWO

"Gamgee!" she burst out. Whenever she had mixed feelings, between gratitude for the ended boredom and blame for impending doom, she thought of the scientist who got her into all this portal rigmarole. The Cessna jarred, her fingers tingled, and her heartbeat soared between the lobes of her ears and the ravaging of the open air by predatory wings.

She pulled up, hoping the wind would tear the beast from her vision.

Cassidy Cane, an archaeologist thirsting for adventure, had gotten into many scrapes over the years. Young by the standards of her faculty — most of them men half again her age — she'd nonetheless run the gamut from the mundane to the exotic.

Crashes were like that. Part thrill, part everyday, and yet a shockingly alien experience. One of the things they don't talk about in the movies is how the senses all suddenly go down different timelines. Her vision had slowed. Everything was almost boring from what she could see. What they wouldn't give back home to see a live pterodactyl! But right now she was just seeing a cockpit and a lizard-bird.

The engine spiralled in an awkward parody of the Doppler effect: that here-and-gone of passing cars. Wind and predators screamed. Her stomach was a centrifuge, and she was glad of her seat — she could feel the spin. Rainforest air, even so high up, was fresh and wild in its scents and even flavours.

The sound of the wing colliding with a flying blade of meat, and the distinct ring of the wing divorcing the plane, came last. It was like seeing a truck go by, looking at a sedan without the front of the car, and then hearing the metallic rending after.

The good news was that the blockage was now free of the window.

Cassidy unbuckled herself from the seat and made a leaning, weaving, bucking series of dashes to the gear nailed and strapped to the back of the plane. Green and blue alternated in the tiny side window she passed. Was the plane careening to the ground like a wheel? She found herself lifting slightly from the floor and ceiling, and "down" became one of those far away, big-picture ideas.

She got to the parachute and had to wedge her hands and feet into the surrounding straps because there was so much spinning in so many directions — punctuated by skrees and meaty thuds — that she climbed more than stood. But this made it difficult to work the straps to get the parachute out. Cursing, she brandished a flip knife and took a steadying breath. Then she cut the straps holding it down, hugged the bundle tight to her left side, and focused on getting the knife re-folded.

Some of the baggage came undone with this hasty unstrapping, and she had to catch a box with her now-free hand — which meant the knife (folded at least) joined the floating dance of bags, bundles, and boxes. She threw the box at the escape hatch, hoping to hit the opening lever and smash out of the plane in a badass dive.

Instead, the box bounced back and bruised her arm before flying off as she slammed into the hatch. "C'mon, you budget bucket of..." She got it open, hung from the edge of the opening because the plane spun again, and slowly hauled herself up with the bruised arm. The spin brought her more and more sidelong to the entrance, and she kicked off the wall to get the last momentum she needed.

She was free!

CHAPTER THREE

She was free!

Her one consolation was that the pterodactyls weren't nipping at her heels. She couldn't tell up from down, though, and didn't know if she had full clearance from the plane. Yet the amount of green she was seeing in her spin meant she was too close to the trees to risk delay. As soon as she had the braces and straps in place, she pulled the cord and the parachute did its thing.

There was so much tearing of branches that all she could do was yell incoherently as she got jerked around even more. So swift and brutal was the swing on breaking through the canopy that the parachute must have caught more tree than air! All the ripping sounds were sickening, and she was so dizzy at this point that she'd have been spinning even if she were lying on the ground.

Dangle.

Breathe.

Wait for the glowing tree trunks to stop orbiting her like a solar system.

Hold up.

"Whoa…" she muttered as soon as she trusted her gut

to stay where it was. How long had she been up here? She couldn't even remember the plane crashing. You'd think a forest would have something to say about a plane crash.

But never mind that.

Many of the trees were glowing! Light was limning intricate slivers through the bark. They reminded her of overhead photographs of highways, slow-exposed so that the headlights smeared into a steady stream of activity. A clear, precise delivery system slowly emerged as she studied them. Absently scratching, she realized she was not in as good repair as the trees.

Blinking a few times, she began a head-to-toe examination. Many twigs were extracted, as well as leaves and some kind of mossy vine. She brushed off some critters and tried not to think about why they were that high in the trees. Lots of cuts. Looking up, the canopy was so thick that her penetration didn't even leave a clear hole. It would have been gloomy, if it weren't for the trees. The light was earthy hues, mostly browns, yellows, and oranges.

It was a warm, honeyed glow. The parachute was hopelessly shredded, and she saw that the ropes were so entangled in the tracery of branches that nothing would be gained from trying to climb them. Her flip knife was lost, but she had others on her person. Never go to other countries, the wilderness, or unexplored portal-dimension-things without multiple knives.

That said, at this height she was going to need a better option than dropping. Beneath her were many extremely large, oddly-shaped bundles of rocks. They looked small from here only because few places on Earth had trees to rival the ones she hung among. The rocks all had spikes, one or two as far as she could see, but rarely in the same place. She took a few moments to rest and prepare herself, through the aching of muscles and lurking emotions (*How am I getting home*?), and swept her gaze around for options.

Plenty of animals, many plants that a botanist would love to see, and nothing she could use. "Okay, um...hello?" she called out.

"Anybody there?"

Despite everything, she was excited. She realized that the portal she'd taken here was roughly pie-shaped, and that her goals were a pie in the sky. She giggled and registered that she had the internal static of being roughed up. Nevertheless, she was all about taking samples home to Gamgee. Real pterodactyls! And trees so large that, even from their lower branches, they went down far enough to look like they were tapering up toward her.

"Huh…" she said with wonder.

Ick!

She managed some awkward fumbling to retrieve from the back of her neck a...bone dart? She drooled out words and all the colours went away.

When she woke up, she felt wonderful. Not goodnight's-sleep wonderful, but finished-a-marathon wonderful. She moved to get in a joyous stretch and instantly cut her luxury short. Her senses flashed open. "Where am I? Why am I tied up?"

"Let the rest do its work," came an odd but soothing voice.

Cassidy looked for its source and laughed. "Oh, I see,

I'm dreaming."

"They say that most times," said the person to her right. "Usually to the humans, though," added the same voice but from an identical body on her left.

The body of a troodon. It looked a little like the Jurassic Park movie version of the velociraptor. Small forearms, the same forward lean and long tail. Even the length and shape of the jaw were similar, though the whole body looked more bird-like than the movie monsters.

She hoped they hadn't taken her phone. There were going to be so many pictures!

"Please do not be alarmed," said one of the troodons. "I am responsible for your treatment."

Cassidy was actually enjoying the feeling of being overwhelmed. It was so rare. "Like a doctor?"

"Most u-halbu have strange words or ways of thinking. But if I understand you rightly, yes," said the other troodon. She was alone with this doctor (for lack of a better word) on a large platform made of intricate and clever weaving techniques. She felt as stable as though she were on flat ground, but the platform was a diamond shape roped with an elaborate suspension system to four dinosaurs — one to a side. All of them were a type she knew little about, called deinocheirus. It was like the super-lizard version of a turkey, but with the arms of a gym enthusiast.

"We tried to give you the usual ear resin," one of the troodons said, "but found that it would not take. Yet we can understand one another. Do you have some illness of the brain?"

"Can you untie me now?" Her brain was digesting

myriads of information on the fly, which was fine, but...
"I figure you'd have killed me already if that's what you
wanted."

As one of the troodons complied, the other replied:
"We were worried about you attacking us. There is little
threat from us, most of the time."

Once her bonds were undone, she was careful not to
startle her host with any sudden moves. He...it...they...
seemed quite calm and collected, but they also felt the
need to tie her down. "Most of the time?"

"There is much for you to learn if you are friendly to
anybody in our community," answered the one that was
tidying up her recent bedding. "We expect, of course, that
you'll connect with the other humans first. They have the
same strange body you do."

Cassidy stared. "You think *I'm* strange?"

The tails of the troodons made a shivering motion. "I
mean no disrespect," they answered together. Cassidy
shivered at the effect.

She kept her eyes firmly on the two troodons, her back
to the edge of the platform. It was like a hovering eleva-
tor. Content to go on carrying it, the deinocheirus showed
no apparent interest in her. "You two talk like you're one
person," she remarked, pointing at each of them in turn.

"They call us the Twin," one of them answered. "About
thirty years ago, our kinds — that is, dinos and humans —
tried an experiment that produced many unusual people
and unexpected results. I'm one of them."

She cast a glance at the wider forest and gasped, only
partly in response to the troodons' unusual medical history. It left her with countless questions that she knew would

be inappropriate to ask, such as what it would mean for the personalities of each of the individual troodons who had entered the experiment. Each of them, she noticed, had an amber headpiece vaguely resembling a headset, but built into the skull.

Though she'd been looking for relief by looking at the forest, it only dominated her calm with its massiveness. The trees were so monumentally large that they needed huge spans of space between the trunks. Yet their branches and leaves intertwined to the point that daylight was more an ambience than a set of rays. There was plenty of space for the mobile platform she rode, and the light came as much from the resonance of amber materials in its construction as it did from the ambience of the surrounding natural world.

The deinocheirus must have each weighed as much as one or two buses, and the four of them had a hip height somewhere between fifteen and twenty feet. The platform she was on could have easily held two dozen patients like how she'd been set up. And the forest was going by at a surreal, sliding pace, far faster than she'd have thought such large beasts of burden could accomplish.

Various quick things scurried between stems, roots, and the legs of the great beasts around her. It was hard to get a good look. Other than that, she never saw much beyond what looked like massive trees and typical wildlife. Yet she hadn't forgotten the bone dart. "Is that why you have those headpieces? I thought they were jewellery." She made conversation. What else could she do?

"What is jewellery?"

Her jaw dropped just a little, but she regained herself.

"They look like amber."

"I suppose they would. And, to an extent, they are. My kind and the humans have worked together for many fires. These," the other troodon used its tail to point at the headpiece of the one speaking, "are how I can be one individual. We're sharing brain matter as one mind."

Frantically, she searched herself.

"Easy now," the Twin said.

Once she found that her tools and weapons were where she'd left them, she swept her eyes over the platform again. Other patients, some human and some dino, occupied the curiously pod-like structures throughout. If there were security measures beyond tying her down, she saw no evidence of them. "You asked about why the work you tried to do on me wouldn't take. What were you trying to do?"

"I see we still have much to discuss," came the reply. "Not long now and we'll be arriving at the nearest gathering. Be at ease. I was trying to give you a temporary translation bulb. Your body would have absorbed it within three days. We do nothing without consent except for the preservation of life and speech."

She began walking all around the platform, her archaeology degree and profession performing parkour in her head. There was cuneiform script on the wooden equipment and even painted onto the dinosaurs. They were about to meet up with the community, as she understood it. "So you would have enabled me to understand you. Is that how you communicate with other dinosaurs and humans?"

"Differences thrive everywhere. Even among my fellow troodons, there are those of us who use different words, think differently, believe at variance." The dip of its head suggested a kind of sadness to her. She had no idea how to read their body language, what messages might be in their eyes or faces. "We do our best to bridge the gaps and survive."

"Do I look like the other humans?"

"No."

"What about my clothes, tools, and such?"

"Not much is obvious to us. We have knives, but generally made of glass or stone. I confess I am feverishly curious. Even your skin looks different. Yet you are unmistakably human."

"You've been awfully patient with my questions," she remarked, "and I'm grateful. But why haven't you asked much, if you're so curious?"

The Twin's troodon arms extended from the chest, with short feathery frills. They weren't as tiny as a T-Rex's in proportion, but they were small enough that much of the rigging of this...facility was in place to assist unusual body types. Nevertheless, the Twin pointed ahead. "There is a process for such things. We'll all have our answers soon enough."

She was sure he — they? — meant that as reassurance and not a threat.

Well, mostly sure.

Cassidy turned to follow the Twin's indication and sure enough, even from where she was, there was obvious evidence of a gathering. The humans were so small that at first she took them for bits of rigging or equipment from this distance. The dinosaurs, of course, were less subtle. She took advantage of the remaining time to rest and collect herself. She'd love to know how they achieved so much strength and stability in what looked to her like ropes and a platform similar to a log cabin. There should have been swaying, at the least.

Easily ten to fifteen feet separated her from the forest floor, but it was patchy. Rocks, holes, knotted roots or dismembered trunks, and even smaller dinosaurs littered her potential landing zones. Occasional rustles and flurries from above – shadows she couldn't place, or caught out of the corner of the eye — told her that the doctor had more security than they were letting on.

On arrival, it took more than an hour for her court session (if that's what this was) to get underway. She finally got a good look at the humans of this arrangement. They all had a Middle-Eastern air, neither Iraqi nor Iranian but more related to those groups than, say, the Saudis. She recalled the mountain below the portal she entered and the wedge-shaped writing. Babylonian?

"She does not have an ear resin," remarked a woman across from Cassidy. Her clothes were similar to robed pictures and paintings Cassidy had seen of Sumerian and Akkadian descent. The legs were distinct, the robes having been redesigned to have pants. They were shortened at the hem and sleeve, with clever weaving for preventing loose folds. Dress was not what set the judges before her apart from anyone else, except that some had specialized tools, straps, belts, and the like for whatever their roles were.

"No, but if I understand this 'Twin,' I don't need it," Cassidy answered with as much poise as she could manage. She was surrounded by dinosaurs big and small, though most were separated by the ring of small fires that had been set up around her and the judges. They hadn't bothered tying her hands or taking her weapons. Their confidence excited her.

The other woman raised a brow. She seemed...impressed? A nod from the troodons confirmed Cassidy's words. The woman pursed her lips as though considering this information, but proceeded. "I am Abnir. I shall be your guide."

"Then you are not a judge?" Cassidy asked. A palpable tension danced along the body language of the humans present.

"We do not know this idea you ask about," Abnir replied, "but be warned: you are to make an account of yourself, not speak with me as an equal."

Cassidy suppressed the urge to grind her teeth at that. Stones had been rolled forth and worked with large plants found nearby. Apparently, the resulting seats suited the three "guides" well enough. Cassidy had been left standing. So she stood. Without further comment.

Abnir's features softened. "Excellent. We have an understanding. Now, tell us about the Deep of the triceratops."

"The what?" Cassidy answered.

"The triceratops are the bulky four-legged—" Abnir began.

"I know them," Cassidy said, "but I d— I apologize for interrupting." Hairs had raised on the back of her neck; she wondered if another dart was aimed at her.

"Then what is the problem?" Abnir prodded with

barely-bridled patience.

"I don't understand what you're asking," Cassidy said, struggling not to study too much of her surroundings. It was obvious that she should have her attention solely on the ju...guides. But she was as afraid as she was intrigued by the dinosaurs and (honestly) wanted more to talk to them. "Some of these..." What should she call them? She gestured at a few of them, making sure to point at a different type every time. "...Are known in my...um... where I'm from."

Abnir seemed skeptical. Her two partners, one male and one female, remained silent and impassive. There were a few snorts, shuffling sounds, mutters, and even a fart from one of the corythosaurus behind her. So little was made of that last noise that Cassidy had to conclude that cultural norms about body sounds were different here. Or maybe some dinos were people while others were beasts?

They waited for her to elaborate.

How could she proceed without asking questions? Surely they'd allow clarification? "What is the Deep?"

Everyone looked at one another — dino and human alike — in consternation. "Just finish her off!" someone shouted.

"I will have the tongue of the next person who says such a thing," Abnir said. Her eyes never left Cassidy's. Cassidy never doubted it. Abnir went on: "The Deep is—" a chorus of roars broke out in the distance. Abnir nodded in that direction. First came the stiff vibrato of a splintering tree, then there was a sound unlike any Cassidy had heard before. It was a blend of Chernobyl and ghost stories.

CHAPTER FOUR

"What was —?" she began.

Abnir held up her hand in a gesture that transcended culture.

Cassidy frowned so hard she almost felt it in her feet.

"Many of us want you dead," Abnir resumed.

Cassidy stared.

"Fortunately for you, I believe as few believe," the leader continued. "Hope must come from elsewhere, delivered from earth or sky."

Crashing sounds, and the unmistakable fleshy thumping of large beasts in combat, sounded from afar. But they grew farther still. Cassidy jerked a thumb in the direction of the noise. "I'm not a lot of reinforcement against whatever that is." Already dim from the canopy, the rainforest was darkening into dusk. It seemed the mood was matching the shadows.

"It grieves us, but this shall have to be cut short," said the man on Abnir's side.

"I will consult the Twin," added the woman opposite him.

"It is planted," Abnir said. Cassidy had to think

through what her translator was not converting: there were metaphors and cultural assumptions at play here. Things that are planted have been fixed in place, and will create their consequences. That, at least, was what Cassidy assumed. Abnir continued: "To the tips of the branches, then — we have witnesses who say you arrived with the shine-wood bird."

Shine-wood? "Do you mean my plane?"

"We do not know this word. We found it dead, but without innards. It was surrounded by wounded and dead dactyls," Abnir added. "Why did it bring you here?"

There were still crashes in the distance. Various wild-life figures screeched or shrieked. It was hard to tell what the sounds belonged to, but they didn't seem to frighten Cassidy's current company. With darkness falling and a surrounding circle of burning mistrust, she was ready to move the process along. "Do you recall the wooden platform that brought me here?" No response. "Well, my machine of 'shine-wood,' as you put it, is like that. It carries people above the ground."

"Much higher than our works," Abnir pointed out. "It flies true."

"Yes," Cassidy replied. "So you see, it doesn't have innards because it's a device. I used it to arrive…" Should she explain what portals were? "…in these lands."

"The Twin told you, I assume, that we have a policy for placing temporary amber on u-halbu so that they can follow our speech?"

"He…er, they…"

Abnir's cohorts shifted in their seats. Their foreheads had a downward tension, and their mouths were thin lines. Abnir, however, was a born leader — graceful (in a hardened way) and concise. "Speak to one of their pair at a time, use 'he.' The Twin is not the only one among us so equipped, but we are not without sympathy for your... misplacement of step."

Beyond the fires, it was hard to see much because of the contrast between struggling light and looming dark. It was sound more than the flow and flight of shadow. The larger dinosaurs either reflected light through scales or hides, or had mounted bundles of luminescent amber. Soon, as though a constellation had come to the ground and become the community, the group was alight with earthy or honeyed glows. Like the trees she'd seen when she (for lack of a better word) landed.

Cassidy nervously watched the proceedings as she fitted words and plans together. There were bundles and platforms, people wrapping themselves in sheets of woven plant, managed fur, and measured hide. They were going to sleep on the move! "Thank you," Cassidy said awkwardly. While the whole settlement tore down or repackaged their set-ups with staggering efficiency, she hoped to sneak in a question: "What do you mean by u-halbu? I don't think I know anything quite like it."

There were people leaping and swinging on vines and ropes above her. Many humans scrambled up rope ladders, got lifted by the dinos, or jumped from trees to get to the backs, saddles, platforms, and other strategies for leveraging the dinosaurs as a means of travel. "It wasn't the triceratops!" someone called from above.

Abnir put her thumb and index finger to her mouth and whistled. Instantly, people and smaller dinos like oviraptors and compsognathus skittered and flitted about. There were corythosaurus, roughly twice the size of Clydesdales, acting like squadron leaders for both humans and the smaller dino groups. Cassidy just took it all in. She noticed that, when they came near her, human hands dwelled on the handles of obsidian knives or whips of a material that might have been leather. When groups of compsognathus, about the size of house cats, flooded by her, it wasn't just a tiny flood of feet. The ones nearest her kept their attention on her. The individuals on the outer edges of their groups watched for other community members or changes in their surroundings. With subtle changes in their tails or how they held their backs, slight changes in their steps or small sounds they made, each sub-group of these clusters communicated to the others.

No one got tripped or stepped on. All items were accounted for. Articles and individuals were secured and organized in remarkable feats of speed and coordination. Cassidy was constantly watched. "It refers to people who are not from the forest," Abnir said amidst the apparent tumult.

The other woman was not escorted. A casual observer might have thought that she and Cassidy were alone amidst a flurry of activity. "Is all the world a forest?" she asked, and it was a multi-pronged question: did they believe so religiously? Had the portal taken her to a forested planet? Were they nomadic, trapped in a prison made of impossible arborous towers and things that screamed when the sun went down?

Abnir's answer came in measured tones and matched her pace. To Cassidy's surprise, the two of them were mounted upon a deinocheirus with the assistance of two human men and a nearby corythosaurus. The latter was chatting with another of its kind at a distance uncomfortable for human conversation. Though she could understand them, she had to concentrate on her co-rider.

"Not all the world is known," Abnir began, "at least not to any one tribe." In a fraction of a second, Cassidy's brain launched fireworks of questions about the organization that Abnir meant by a tribe. Were humans and dinos separate tribes? Was this whole group one tribe? How much meeting and cooperation — or competition — was there? Member transplantation? Territory? But she could not interrupt her guide/ judge, who didn't miss a beat: "Yet there is the forest as a physical thing, and then there is the forest as greater truth. But none of this is your question," she remarked, looking over her shoulder to smile at Cassidy.

The archaeologist was reminded of intelligentsia and investors she'd met in numerous circles of power. Hunting for grant money, university conferences that were really thinly-veiled recruitment strategies, festivals of ego and threat arranged by the bigwigs for no other purpose than to have lips applied to their hindquarters. Abnir would have appeared to them as primitive because they wouldn't have looked at her properly, but this woman was the sort of figure who could sharpen her tongue on the mirror of Helen of Troy.

Cassidy smiled back.

Abnir elaborated without any obvious acknowledgement of the exchange, but a shift had occurred. "You must be thinking that if we were going to kill you, we'd have done so." Cassidy felt the question in her fingertips, but didn't need to respond. "I figure much the same. You will notice we relieved you only of your damaged harness."

Blinking, Cassidy quickly checked herself. She'd been so focused on physical injury, possible violence, and social dangers that her clothes only mattered for comfort. The contents of her pockets and pouches mattered more. "Many are the strange things about you," Abnir continued, "but as you see: we know a harness when we see one."

It was time to risk a question. Cassidy asked, "Did you train the dinosaurs? Many of them seem quite clever. How many of them are people?"

She didn't get an immediate opportunity to ask Abnir about the other woman's tension because their mount stopped and swivelled her neck around. Cassidy was looking the massive creature in the eye, and it felt like sliding down the pebbled side of a mountain. "Why would any of us not be people?" This was a deep-chested being with singular muscles larger than everything Cassidy was. It was like the angry moan of a bull, turned into a reptile's piping force and enlarged many times over.

Cassidy was a soda can that had been stepped on.

"I...I'm sorry," she stammered.

"Never mind the offence," the lumbering being replied. "I want to know."

Cassidy processed that for a moment. The rest of the community (tribe?) continued about their business. No one was worried for Abnir, it seemed, and none of them were going to wait. "What's your name?" asked the archaeologist, in the hopes that it would help somehow.

"Belessunu," the deinocheirus replied. She still hadn't resumed walking.

It occurred to Cassidy that she didn't have to go into explanations about other worlds, dimensions, or portals. They'd seen her plane, perhaps even the "battle" (to put it generously). But did they see her come out of the earthy hole in the sky? "Where I'm from," she started carefully, "the only evidence of dinosaurs are remains. Bones, mostly." Well, fossils, but she wasn't getting into that. She wondered absently if they lumped the dinosaurs together wholesale; if she was just misunderstanding the terms they used based on her assumptions, and where their marks of separation might be. But she didn't lose verbal stride: "The bones were far larger than most — if not all — of the animals any of my people had ever heard of. But still, they were more like in shape to animals than to pe... humans. So you see…"

"Humans are the only ones with intelligence where you're from," Belessunu finished for Cassidy. She started walking again. They were now closer to the end of the line of the group. Abnir, in front of Cassidy, kept her gaze straight ahead and made no comment.

Striving to hide her concern, Cassidy took up the conversation. "I meant no disrespect."

"I understand," the deinocheirus replied. "We must be frightfully new to you, then."

You have no idea.

"And big," Cassidy said. Belessunu nodded. With the size of her head and the relative haste of her stride — she was gradually inching her way back up the line — the deinocheirus moved both ponderously and quickly. It was as surreal as encountering a blizzard the very first time one has seen snow. After a pause, she risked another question: "Where are we going?"

"We're moving," Belessunu answered, as though this were the most obvious thing in the world.

"Yes, but where?"

Belessunu sharply turned her head so she could regard Cassidy as though the human was daft, but set her gaze forward and focused on navigating the group, the trees, and the terrain. They entered a span of trees like the ones Cassidy had seen on first arrival, with the limning bronze-ish light. Abnir turned around and said, "Let me teach you."

They spent some time moving and re-working the (to give it a name) saddle-like contraption that occupied so much of the back of the deinocheirus. It could have easily seated a dozen humans, with other accommodations clearly intended for smaller dino varieties as well. Yet the two of them were the only occupants, made all the more conspicuous by Belessunu's sheer size.

Cassidy spoke little because the guide was keeping up the conversation to show her how everything worked and why, and to help her move back a bit and re-adjust so that both of them could be secured. They now faced one another. Some of the adjustments involved clever interwoven ropework so studiously arranged that it acted solid, like a bamboo vine. Working with them, despite her youth and athleticism, took enough effort that Cassidy was breathing heavily at several points throughout their lesson.

Only when they were restored to proper and secure seating, and Belessunu had returned them to the front of the line, could they readily resume conversation. At which point Abnir still had to coordinate the activities of the group and field questions. Food and water were passed along. Cassidy accepted what she was given with gratitude and hoped that there weren't any germs or parasites to which she might be vulnerable. It wasn't like Gamgee and the rest of the team back home could prepare vaccines for a new dimension!

While she waited for Abnir to be able to pick up where they'd left off, she watched everyone's efforts, roles, tools, techniques, and behaviours. She had to be quick — it didn't look like they'd finished with her little tribunal earlier. In the back of her mind, other questions were bouncing around. Dinosaurs lived in conditions very different from the modern human Earth she knew. Oxygen, temperature, possibly even pressure, moisture, and the kinds of gases in the air were all different in their day. She couldn't recall anyone showing fossil evidence that dinosaurs had anything resembling speech, and certainly not the brainpower for culture, names, and language!

She watched and she wondered. Many people were smoking. None of them were close enough for her to smell it or engage with them, but it didn't look like any cigarette or cigar she'd ever seen. In fact, they were green tubes and reminded her of the veins of a leaf. Abnir finally returned her attention to the archaeologist. "I didn't understand your question earlier." They reached the visual edge of the towering, lighted trees and turned. It wasn't quite a reversal, but more like they were keeping a respectable distance from the dark.

Cassidy pointed. "Are we staying in the lighted areas

during the night?"

"Of course. You cannot see danger in the shadows."

"Where is your community?"

Blank stare.

Cassidy rolled her hands as she tried to find a way to express her question. "I see that you've built beds for people on the move." Abnir nodded slowly, her eyes darting from one side to another. She clearly didn't see where the archaeologist was going with this. "So where are your still beds?"

"Are you asking how we deal with our dead?"

"Heavens, no!" Cassidy sat up straighter. "Where do you lie down for the night?"

As though the other woman were an idiot, Abnir again pointed at the bed platforms and saddles with rigging for the smaller dinosaurs.

A conclusion was tugging at Cassidy's brain like a child urgently pulling on a sleeve. "Where do the larger dinosaurs sleep?"

"In groups, guarded by other dinos and humans. We are attentive, we stay well-armed. The lazy cannot contribute." Cassidy knew the word as "lazy" because of the effects of her translator, but she thought she caught something and refused to believe it. "Say that bit about dealing with your dead again."

Abnir's expression was dangerous.

"It's not what you think!" Cassidy quickly clarified, holding up her hands in self-defence. "Please, humour me."

"Are you asking how we deal with our dead?"

"No, the other part — about contribution." Cassidy

wasn't blinking. She must have sounded delirious. But after a moment's hesitation…

"The lazy cannot contribute."

It was true: the words for lazy and dead were the same in their language!

Cassidy wiped the sweat from her brow. She was lightly dressed for travel, but thoroughly covered. She hadn't expected the night to be this warm. Despite their colossal size, the trees felt close and crowded. There was a whistle from somewhere along the line, but it couldn't have been made with human lips. The archaeologist witnessed a changing of the guard. They were moving in shifts!

She turned her attention back to Abnir. "You never stop."

"Is that a question?"

"More or less."

"We meet up with other tribes from time to time. There is trade. We've been sundered from others of our group because of the last Deepening. You found the triceratops sleeping it off. And we have work platforms, though those are repurposed for medicine or sleep depending on need or time of day. I hope you won't judge us harshly; you've crossed our path where it is well mucked."

Why would she care what I think of her? Cassidy was taken aback. She was also exhausted. "So then…"

"You should rest," Abnir interrupted.

"No, but…" Cassidy had been feeling the fatigue for hours already. Adrenaline, fascination, and the awareness of some obscure danger they weren't talking about kept her going. "How long was I with the Twin?"

"Since early yesterday. He worked on you overnight.

We had to compel him to rest when he arrived at the council with you. He was the only true healer to survive the last Deepening."

Cassidy slept, and didn't even know it was coming.

She leapt up, sleep still in her eyes, and blinked rapidly while she turned to and fro.

"Are you well?" There were a few other humans on the platform, but the speaker got her attention.

"The Twin!"

Both troodons tilted their heads. "Yes?" they said together. Then again, "Are you all right?"

"I…" she started, and checked herself. "I think so." She then spent some time on the cricks and stiffness in her muscles and joints. "It's been a while since I've been that tired."

"Is that why you slept so long? Are you prone to that?"

She didn't stop limbering up. At this point, Cassidy had accepted that feeling normal wasn't in the cards. "Same as most people, eight-ish hours."

"You must have a relaxed world," the Twin said. One of the troodons had sat back, plopping down with his tail and two legs spreading out equally. Cassidy giggled, as it looked ridiculous. Only the standing troodon spoke, but he did so with such awe that Cassidy forgot the antics of the Twin's other half and stared at him.

"What do you mean?" she asked.

"More than four hours at a rest seems an awful lot. We have guarded you so long only because the revered Abnir has high hopes for you."

She turned and regarded Abnir, who was at the other

end of the platform, in what appeared to be a small meeting with the two other guides from the circle of fire. "Wait, how did I get onto this platform? We were on the...I mean, we were riding...we were with Belessunu."

"When you passed your fifth hour with no sign of waking," the Twin explained, "you were sent to me."

CHAPTER FIVE

Part of Cassidy's mind, accustomed as she was to taking in all her surroundings and processing many details at once, registered that many of the humans in the group were smoking again. Daylight was as strong as it was likely to get. None of this stretch looked the same as the rainforest of last night, though it all sort of looked the same and different times of day could change a surprising amount of the landscape. She never missed a beat: "You never sleep more than four hours?"

"Some of the large dinos do, but triceratops don't have as many weaknesses and predators as you humans do. That is, after all, one of the things you gain from us. Now that you mention it, humans do generally get six to ten hours throughout a given day. But all at once? No chance."

That made sense. Well, as much as anything made sense in a place where humans and dinosaurs could talk and breathe the same air. "It seems," she started, trying to find the right words, "that you and I come from very different communities. I'm used to places where we can settle long enough to build. Not just tools and things like this platform," she spread her hands out to indicate where they were, and noticed a strange cluster of indentations in one corner that never much registered before, "...but whole buildings." When she saw the uncomprehending light in the Twin's eyes, she tried a different take on the concept. "We built containers, like solid pouches or boxes, big enough for people to live in."

Abnir had rejoined them, but did not interrupt. Her wonderment at Cassidy's wild tale of houses and sleeping in one spot was as complete as the Twin's. "Even in your sleep," she continued, "you have to keep moving?" Abnir nodded. Cassidy registered that the trees were starting to show signs of that telltale glow again. She pointed. "Why do they do that?"

"The glow?" the Twin clarified. At Cassidy's nod, Abnir took up the explanation: "The dinos have helped us humans with all manner of ideas, as well as their physical work. Our size and body type comes with its own advantages. We work together in all things, and building a resin network is one of them. Most of our tools, materials, and abilities come from our studies of the ambers and resins."

"That must mean that you alter as many trees as you can, whenever you have the luxury of stopping long enough to work on the trees," Cassidy remarked.

Abnir shook her head. "We have to begin the process straight from the seeds," the Twin said. "The amount of work to change a tree already grown is well past any hope of safety."

Cassidy was fascinated. "Some of these trees are huge! They'd have needed centuries to grow!"

"Yes," the Twin said.

Abnir added, "We have not learned how to alter the seeds past their own generations, though."

Cassidy frowned. She'd registered that she needed to relieve herself. She also noticed that humans were using the strange indentations every once in a while to do just that. She supposed it was logical: the dinosaurs acted like horses when it came to nature's call. Why would the humans feel any shame, and how would it be practical to keep moving if they did? While she mustered the courage to go about her business in full view of everyone, she continued the conversation: "Do you mean you can't get the new trees to keep making seeds that will produce the light?"

"We cannot get them to produce seeds at all," Abnir answered.

"You'll notice that even the most densely lighted patches still have unlit trees," the Twin said.

Cassidy, unable to hold it any longer, went about her business. Abnir and the Twin began conversing about their various responsibilities and plans. She had to wait to rejoin them while they concluded their management. Then she picked up again: "How long has it been since you could create such wondrous uses for the sap?"

"Countless generations," Abnir answered easily.

"Why do you ask?" the Twin said.

"I just…" she pointed in various directions. "I see a lot of rainforest that goes for many…" she faltered while she tried to phrase distance, "…days without the glowing resin. Shouldn't all of it be covered by now?"

Again, one of the bodies of the Twin seemed to fall in

a child-like exhibition of shock. Abnir, equally astounded, was the one to find her voice: "You expected even more? That any have survived — never mind whole groves of light — is a source of great pride to us."

"Forgive me," Cassidy said, trying to match their gravity. "I see that I am accustomed to much more safety than you are." Both of the others offered a solemn bow, and she mimicked it — if only in an attempt to show respect. "We also have different takes on space," she reflected aloud, "and I don't quite follow some of your reasoning. You all keep together as though you have a purpose or destination, but you just sort of...keep going."

"The only stillness we understand for the living is to be a plant or be dead," the Twin said.

"That's our next 'purpose,' if I understand how you're using the word," Abnir rejoined. "We call it utuki, and mostly we smoke it. We want it because we enjoy it, but we must also destroy it."

"There's a lot to that," Cassidy mused aloud.

"There is," the Twin confirmed. "We dinos dislike the plants, though we don't know why. There are slate outcroppings we've encountered where our young will scrape their claws. The sound has a similar feeling." Cassidy resisted the urge to laugh: nails on a chalkboard was a strange cultural bonding point! He answered before she could ask: "It isn't just that the humans like the flower. Utuki make the glow-trees sick, and much of our toolery comes from glow-tree sap."

Toolery? She knew he meant technology. This translation phenomenon was strange. It got across what they meant, despite having nothing in common in terms of the roots of the languages. It's not like there was any Greek or Latin influence in these people. In fact, they reminded her of stories of ancient Babylon. It was like the jumping of the language barrier used her knowledge as a frame of reference.

She also realized there were no trees with the telltale luminous resin lines. And that the people around her were arming up far more than they had against her.

"What's going on?" she asked.

"We've shared a great deal with you, given that you're the one under suspicion," Abnir said. She stood casually, relaxed, as though her role in the proceedings was over and others were taking up the operations. Cassidy wondered at the odd friendly-hostile dynamic here. Abnir went on: "Many of us, Belessunu included, wanted to end you straight off because you came to us amid a flight of dactyls."

Cassidy let her jaw drop at that.

"Abnir believes we need outside help to win the wars we wage," the Twin said. Each troodon was operating independently, speaking with compsognathus and humans alike as he coordinated the rigging for a mobile battle-hospital arrangement.

There was so much to learn! Before Cassidy could form a question, though, Abnir's commanding but calm tones demanded attention: "You built your wings, or someone from your community did so. My scouts heard you before they saw you. They saw there was smoke. Your wings and your clothes, and even your tools and equipment, are made of materials we've never seen. Your toolery is strange. How came you among the dactyls?"

Her pride chafing at this shift in handling her, Cassidy said, "I'm not a bucking stallion, and we're going in the same direction — at least for now. Pick a stance already." Abnir's eyes had an almost visible sheen of indignation and outrage shimmer through them. Cassidy made no apology for her mouth getting ahead of her, and didn't even lose stride. "I wasn't among them. They attacked me as soon as I was within reach of them. It all happened so fast, I wasn't sure what to make of it. They did a lot of what I thought was screaming. Were they angry? Did I do something wrong, just going about my business in the air?"

"We're not used to humans having business in the air," the Twin remarked. The troodon that hadn't spoken made a scaly barking noise that eventually registered as laughter. She realized he was trying to cut the tension in the air.

The human leader was ambaric. Such was the stillness in her poise and the feeling, like static electricity, of her sheer presence. Her silence was on the cusp of long before she decided to pick a stance — for now. "That does sound like the dactyls. We've long ago come to the conclusion that they have a kind of intelligence, though they are not people by any measure we know," Abnir said with some disgust. Cassidy was vaguely reminded of stories she'd heard in her homeworld of dragons. "Dactyls are beasts, destroyers from the skies. They mostly stay above the canopy, because the forest protects the people who learn to love and protect it in turn."

Cassidy had her doubts about that conclusion, but didn't voice them. In fact, she didn't get much chance to voice anything: she realized that the darkness had thickened here. The canopy was denser, the air here close and tight, and a cacophony of lungs, feet, and wings lunged at them from beyond their sight.

Many of the larger dinos spread out and lowered the platforms they were carrying. All this time Cassidy thought they were for tools and resources: it looked like rock, bark, possibly obsidian or other forms of volcanic glass. Instead, many of those "stones" stood up as the platform lowered! Humans around her laboured alongside smaller dinos to leverage massive wooden contraptions. They were too odd to have been obvious to her while she was occupied in discussion, but these were arbalests and dino-mounted ballistae!

Some of the platforms also featured things made largely out of wood and amber, and she had no idea what they were. The dinos who'd stood away from these contraptions — the same ones she thought were boulders — turned out to be ankylosaurus. These were like the dino equivalent of badgers. Though bulky, they stayed low on all fours and seemed resolute and immovable. Unlike badgers, these bony-shelled living tanks had sizeable tails that ended in a wrecking ball. They marched forward, and not a moment too soon.

Stegoceras rampaged and stampeded out of the dark!

They were two-legged and most of their size was in their length. They weren't as low as alligators, and not much shaped like the more familiar creature, but they were big when compared to humans. Their heads had natural bone helmets, which they used for ramming. Though any one of them were no match for the deinocheirus and other larger dinos in this group, the stegoceras were a flood of dry carnage. They ran, they rammed, and they wrought.

Several corythosaurus went down.

Even as they fell, human and dino fought together. Human tools and contraptions fired bundles of fire and some — once they burst — appeared to be acid. Spears and other shaft-like weapons were launched from ballistae and the like. Dactyls joined the fray, throwing everything into chaos. Humans were plucked up to be eaten or dropped, devices were rent asunder, dinos were attacked in the eyes or pulled off the backs of larger dinos. It was then that the amber "toolery" was put to use.

Cassidy fell to the platform, each of the troodons of the Twin working to protect her and Abnir. The amber weapons launched sonic blasts! Waves of sound, dense enough to be briefly visible, passed through the dactyls. For a fraction of a second, Cassidy thought there was no resistance, but then she registered that every one of them lost flight from the wave. Additional amber blasts, flattened and widened when aimed downward, tossed the stampeding stegoceras like toys lined up in front of a newly activated industrial fan.

"We should be quick," someone said as he landed on the platform next to the trio.

"What? Why?" asked Cassidy. She was the first to regain herself.

The man was not alone. He and the others, along with some oviraptors, were carrying sacks and backpacks. They were using some kind of gliding getup made with a membrane Cassidy didn't immediately recognize. And rope. Lots of rope. Abnir was up quickly, and the Twin focused upon incoming wounded. "They're harvesting utuki before we set it all alight," Abnir explained. "You should—"

"Let me go with them!" Cassidy wasn't passing up this opportunity.

Doubt bounced between Abnir and the collectors, but there wasn't much time. "I'll want a report, Eshkar," she told the man.

He nodded once, tossed Cassidy an extra sack, and his team set to work. They didn't waste words. Cassidy kept up with them to a point that seemed to surprise them. They leapt and swung down the lengths of rope and elaborate dino harnesses with almost superhuman ease, whereas she kept it simple and not quite as graceful. Still, she'd done enough adventuring that ropes and ladders and the like — no matter how oddly configured — were like a second home to her.

It was like the running of the bulls.

The trees were so large that, now they were away from their larger dinosaur friends, the humans had to dodge using the massive roots. A tree trunk isn't a quick go-around when it's more than forty feet wide. Blasts of fire quickly caught with the underbrush, so there was a slithering black-orange contrast that made details harder to catch. Some of the stegoceras came and went so quickly that it was like the darkness itself gave and took their forms.

"Watch your left!" Cassidy called out to one of them as she jumped for the cover of a mushroom the size of a pickup truck.

He didn't even look: the man dove into a roll to his right, and a stegoceras foot clomped on the ground where he'd stood a fraction of a second earlier. He didn't bother calling out thanks, and she didn't wait for it. A blast, wide and loud, raked the ground ahead of them as one of the amber guns took out a wave of the rogue dinos.

CHAPTER SIX

Eshkar ducked. Cassidy poked her head out enough to watch him, lit by a nearby fire, as he gathered a four-pointed flower. His cohorts had spread out, avoiding the fire, and the ones most in the smoke held something to their faces. A cluster of compsognathus wove between the hardheaded stegoceras and had nowhere else to go but to flow over the next patch of flowers.

The ground urged as though it would throw up with all the shifting and stamping of the larger dinos. A deinocheirus, its leg broken by a group of reckless and determined stegoceras, crashed hard into a tree. Cassidy heard a sound she couldn't believe: the breaking of a bone. A bone the size of a cement mixer. Unforgettable, the sound was somewhere between the sharp crack of a splitting glacier and the wet smack of a massive tree hitting something hard.

Colours swarmed Cassidy's vision, and for an instant she thought the bones were hers.

"U-halbu!" she heard Eshkar cry out. Shaking her head, she ran forward again, following the curve of the mushroom. "Don't!" he shouted, but it was too late: she slid to a stop in front of the compsognathus.

They were like angry, cat-sized lizards. They'd been helping the community not ten minutes ago. But now they looked at her with a primal cross of hunger and revenge. Thinking quickly, she dug a magnesium flare out of her leg pouch, watched the creatures eye-to-eye as the little dinos stepped in clumsy unison toward her, and lit the flare with her free hand. They screamed when its vicious light took hold. Cassidy took a certain satisfaction from the impressed and frightened sounds of the human collectors behind her, and flung the flare into the mushroom next to her.

It was slobbering flame and spores even as she turned.

She ran.

A wooden stake slammed into the ground to her right, a skewered dactyl still twitching at its end. Her legs wrestled with the acidic tension of weight and haste. A fleshy landing thumped on her left. People cried out in pain, triumph, fear. Dinos let out roars and vibratos, shrieks and gulps and snarls.

Cassidy saw a patch of the flowers sheltered between two roots of a massive tree that was being ignored several large dinos away. Smoke billowed and stegoceras bellowed. She jogged, and did her best to sway in imitation of the dark plant stalks that sprouted up here and there. A dactyl crashed and slid by her, but the teeth marks in it suggested that it had been tossed — not that it was diving at her.

She filled her pouch, but didn't do any harm to the remaining flowers. Several of them blossomed so quickly that she did a double-take, but they didn't seem to do anything else. Her stomach leapt as though there'd been a big G-force change in an odd direction, but she managed to lurch back the way she came without too much issue. It was getting harder to tell foe from lesser foe. In the back of her mind, she wondered if the dactyls were some kind of albatross. Had they goaded the stegoceras into attacking?

Cries and shouts rang out above. Shattered amber landed a good hard run ahead of her, but she made no effort in that direction. Instead, she pivoted, heading for what would be the rear of the dino-human caravan that had taken her here. She climbed a mound of something she couldn't make out in the confusing darkness and fire-light, but it felt fleshy and she thought it might have been green if she could have seen it.

It was too late to stop when she went far enough over the mound to practically land on a stegoceras. So she embraced the situation and straight-up landed on the bipedal ramming beast. It wasted no time running for all it was worth. Her arms were wrapped around the base of its neck. Wind held her legs aloft with the dino's momentum. Had she startled it? Was it trying to shake her off, escape the melee, or hunt something down?

A huge foot thumped nearby, hard enough for the stegoceras to lose its footing. Cassidy pulled and let go for all she was worth so that her momentum carried her well past the stumbling beast. She rolled into the landing on what turned out to be a slight upward slope of the ground. To her surprise, she was able to roll out of it running. A rope dangled from a corythosaurus and she managed to clamber her way up.

"Hi!" she said, once she was mounted. "I'm Cass."

"Mashda," the corythosaurus replied. "Did you get your flowers?"

"Yep; got separated."

"Clearly."

"Do you think you could get me back to Abnir?"

"Possibly," Mashda said. "But first: did you see any resin toolery? Some of it fell."

"Yes," Cassidy answered, a little nonplussed. "It's up there, past the burning mushroom. Why?"

"We'll need to get what we can. Hold on." And she was off.

Cassidy ran with it. Questions later.

Once Mashda brought her abreast of the crumble of amber, Cassidy had to jump off to help two of the humans from the collection group and another corythosaurus gather it together and bundle it into a kind of dumbwaiter setup attached to the side of a deinocheirus. "Where's Eshkar?" Cassidy called to one of the humans while she worked.

"Had to regroup," he answered. "He's with the dactyl fighters now. I saw him fend them away from…" he was cut off as three more ramming skulls came their way. A wooden battering ram swung down sidelong and took them all out at once. Shocked, Cassidy turned and looked up. It had been mounted on a second deinocheirus, a rope and pulley system working it from the side of what she now realized was Belessunu. "Nice shot!" she waved up.

"Thank you," Belessunu said with a shuffle of her head.

Cassidy was being helped up the length of the

deinocheirus before she knew what was happening. Soon she stood beside Abnir again, the other woman limping on a bandaged leg. A flurry of dactyls went up beyond the canopy. As the monstrous trunks of the trees swung in the extremes of Cassidy's vision, she realized they were on a turn.

"We're retreating?" she asked no one in particular.

Eshkar was by her side. He looked vaguely Iranian — like the others — and his hair was kept short. Between their appearances and the wedged writing system they used, it occurred to Cassidy that they might even be Sumerian. The site where they'd found the portal was, some argued, the place of the Tower of Babel in ancient days. But surely her mind was running on without her. She pulled herself back to the tasks at hand.

Blood, dirt, and a telltale gleam of a varnish over Eshkar's skin told her there was more to him and his team than she first thought. In the vanishing firelight, she noticed that several people were coated in this resin. Eshkar answered her: "The dactyls seek reinforcements. We want to be well out of thought by the time they arrive. We got a good supply. Your eye is sharp: you picked good samples."

"Thanks," she said.

And without another word, she set about working on the rest of the platform. At first she helped with some basic debriefing and cleanup tasks, and she spread what food she'd had from her rations among the group. They sniffed at it at first, but ate soon enough. The rest of her work was with the Twin. Medical wasn't her field, but she took every opportunity to help with triage, field dressings, moving people, and using some of the tech. The troodons explained to her whenever the Twin had a mouth or some hands free. She wasn't exactly an X-ray tech, but they did have (and showed her how to use) a strange bathing device made of worked amber parts that glistened and shivered.

She was reminded of a cat purring. "It uses a sound that helps with healing," the Twin explained.

Abnir was in and out to receive reports and give instructions, but largely congregated with Eshkar and his team of what Cassidy thought were some kind of scouts. Once the humans were sorted out, she wasted no time in requesting and receiving assistance getting to the platforms used for the dinos. The Twin came with her, leaving his assistants to keep an eye on the patients. Cassidy laboured for their aid because she didn't really know what was happening, but she knew this: pain and loss bring everyone together.

Hands drifted away from obsidian knives as the night went on. Dinos stopped watching her for danger and started watching her methods, her state of exhaustion, her attempts to learn their ways.

She took a turn of her own in the resin healing pool. She could have sworn she'd only blinked, but the darkening night was now so punctured by slivers of white sunlight that she had to accept that it was daytime. "Is it noon?" she asked. She couldn't believe the brightness. She was also surprised by how much her tongue stuck to the roof of her mouth while she spoke.

"Ah, yes, well risen," the Twin replied. One of him was adjusting the settings of her pool while the other troodon was holding a discussion with Abnir a few feet away. If Cassidy cared to pick out the words, she could have, but it took more focus than she could muster right now.

"Uh, well risen to you," she said. "How long was I out?"

"I was told you had gotten in about an hour before dawn," he answered. "So at a guess: six hours or so. How do you feel?"

"Wonderful," she answered, and caught herself off-guard with just how true that was. "It's like I've had all the benefits of a hard workout, full rest, stretching, massage, and yoga," she finished. "I'll need one of these for my bedroom."

"You are using many terms I do not know," the Twin said.

Right.

"Never mind," she said, and she was halfway through dressing before she realized that she'd fallen into this culture's attitudes about nudity. Extra warmth made its way to her face, but her glances didn't uncover any unusual (or untoward) attention. "Wait: did you leave me in that all night?"

"Clearly."

"Isn't that well in excess of...I mean, you have so many others..."

The Twin let out that laugh-bark. "Usually, yes, but you've done much to ingratiate yourself. And you had a somewhat chafing welcome."

She shrugged. "Trust me, I've dealt with much worse."

"I don't doubt it," he replied confidently.

Cassidy tugged at and smoothed out her clothes some more, and focused on them. "Hey," she said, "why do my clothes feel funny?"

"We did what we could," Abnir answered. Cassidy stood straighter and faced the other woman, who was still dirty. She'd had sleep, but little else; her eyes were tight, sharp, and edged with premature wrinkles. She studied Cassidy as she spoke: "Your hides and fabrics are strange to us. But we are grateful for your help."

"Of course," Cassidy responded. She looked around as the caravan came to a halt. There was no sign of dactyls, and she was surprised to see several stegoceras being treated on a different platform. One of the troodons was talking with someone who'd just swung over from there, while the other was still with Abnir and Cassidy. She registered absently that the troodons never went beyond ten feet of each other if they could help it, and often kept less than five.

"I brought you this," Abnir said. Most of the others in the caravan, as far as Cassidy could tell at a glance, were resting. Abnir was holding out one of the tubes the others had been smoking. Many of the ones resting — the humans, at least — were preparing to do just that.

Though most were trying to play it cool, Cassidy could tell that everyone felt a certain awe but a pressure not to pay too much attention. She wasn't surprised: having a leader personally present a gift, regardless of its scale, was considered a great honour in many cultures. She didn't smoke, but this also was clearly not tobacco. "I...I'm touched by your generosity," she managed. She accepted it gingerly.

She'd noticed that there were no ankylosaurus in evidence, but couldn't remark on that just yet. She turned the stalk about this way and that, making no effort to hide her inspection. Abnir said, "We make it entirely using the utuki. Even the stalk is made by an art of the utuki stem." Sure enough, Cassidy recognized seams and portions in the tube-shaped object: it was an unusual weaving technique.

As she spoke, Abnir retrieved something that looked like a small coconut from one of her aides. There was a hole in it, continuously producing a tiny column of flame. "How…?" Cassidy asked as Abnir lit her flower-stalk and passed the coco-flame to her.

Abnir's lips quirked on one side as Cassidy accepted the flame and availed herself. "Even were I to pass you to each of my people and the dinos in turn, for a year apiece, I doubt we could teach you all there is to be said for our ways, tools, plants, and animals. Could you teach me everything, even just about your wings, if I came to your home?"

Cassidy smirked in turn. "Not a chance. And thank you." She took her first puff of the utuki.

And sat down hard.

A chorus of laughter washed over her. Oddly, she could taste the laughter. It was like macaroni and cheese, if each noodle carried a different flavour. Steak, french fries, oregano, blueberries, kale. She smelled colours. Her whole body awareness got blended in with her surroundings. Then everything snapped back. She was woozy, but somehow back on her feet, and there was nothing in her hands.

"I'm sorry," Abnir said without being sorry at all, "I couldn't resist. Most of us have been smoking whenever we could since we were old enough for moonblood. An adult who'd never tried it…"

Cassidy coughed. Her eyes watered. She felt like a five-year-old who'd taken a shot of something that was whiskey mixed with something that was not. Charges would have been laid where she was from, and for good reason, but those laws she knew were no good here. At least this meant they accepted her? "Don't worry about it," she rasped.

The Twin shuffled nervously. It was a little surreal seeing the same emotion play out in the same way between two different bodies, especially knowing that they had the same mind. It dawned on her to ask, but Belessunu, striding nearby, lowered her head enough to join the conversation: "Smoking is a human thing. The utuki works differently for you. We don't understand how you could enjoy it."

Cassidy stopped herself from agreeing with the deinocheirus. "None of the dinos smoke?"

"None."

"Never?"

"Never. Just being around those plants gives us the shivers." Belessunu watched as a cluster of ankylosaurus crested a small embankment. "They're here."

Abnir went to the edge of the platform, near the body of one of the deinocheirus carrying it, and got some assistance from some of the other humans as she made her way down an elaborate rope ladder setup. "She's expected to greet lost members of the group when they come in

big numbers or belong to the same spines," the Twin remarked for Cassidy's benefit. "Should it come up in song,
I do not care for this smoking practice."

She tried to parse that.

"Our different kinds have different backbones," Belessunu answered the confused human's expression. "Your
idea of lumping all dinos and all humans into two groups
is a little unnatural, though perhaps not so much. Humans
are, after all, very strange."

"I won't deny that," Cassidy smirked. The others
laughed, or made sounds that she now knew were laughter. But she had more questions. "Why do you seek out
the plants at all?"

"They harm the glow-trees," Belessunu said. "A sickness spreads from them. It does nothing to the normal
trees, but it's a threat to our way of life."

Cassidy saw more benefit from the resinous technology for the humans than for the dinos, but wouldn't risk
coming across as arguing the point. Besides, she was human herself — she was likely privileged or otherwise bi-
ased. It made sense to her to wait for the ankylosaurus to
catch up, but… "How did the ankylosaurus get left behind?"

"They're rearguard," the Twin explained. Cassidy
watched as they were examined, information was exchanged, and the process began in earnest to bring them
up with the platforms. Witnessing this slow and careful
procedure, and remembering the chaos of the double attack of the dactyls and the stegoceras, everything fit into
place for her. Besides, it's not like anybody could harm
the heavily-armoured dinos. They were simply too slow

to catch up. When lined up and well-placed, though, they were an impenetrable wall.

"How many did we lose?" Cassidy berated herself for not thinking to ask about that earlier.

Silence.

She looked at the other two. Neither would meet her gaze. Eventually, she said, "Forgive me."

Both nodded. Neither spoke.

Eshkar joined them. Belessunu, called upon as a deinocheirus to assist with the caravan responsibilities, said, "To the march," and turned away.

"We'll be ready to move once the ankylosaurus are secured," Eshkar said. "Abnir sends her congratulations: it was a successful weeding."

Cassidy stared. People and dinos died in order to kill some flowers? What was going on?

"Have there been any signs?" the Twin asked.

"None," said Eshkar. "One of the ankylosaurus Deepened in the midst of battle, but she was far from the others, so we..."

We what?

Cassidy didn't risk asking, but the Twin and some of his nearby assistants who were in earshot all nodded in grim understanding. She had a different insight: "Do the dactyls get the Deep?"

The Twin turned to his duties. She wondered if she'd offended him, or if he was just overburdened. Eshkar took on her guidance: "I'd never thought to ask that myself. Our myths and legends tell us of a sap that came from the sea and split apart, some of it becoming amber. The rest became song. Some say that music is a part of the world, and was there before us. It will be there when we are gone. There are many stories that connect the dactyls with these histories, but each tribe sings differently about this."

Cassidy digested all of that. "I would be grateful if I could learn your stories sometime. Maybe after I've figured out how I'll get home, I could come back. If you'd let me?"

"It is not for me to make such a ruling," Eshkar said. "But I do love the resinfire."

"The what?"

"A festival of story between tribes. It's too big a discussion to get into right now, but later…" he said.

"Later," she agreed. "Do humans get nothing like the Deep?" she asked, careful to keep her voice too low for any nearby dinos to hear.

He studied her for an uncomfortably long time. Was he wrestling with something internally? Making decisions about her? Considering social or cultural implications? She was about to retract her question or change the subject when he said, "Not exactly. With the dinos, it seems to be random. Once there is Deepening, it's important to get them away from the others, because sometimes they seem to catch it from the ones in the Deep. But there's never been a pattern that we could congeal." She realized he meant there was nothing they could nail down, but their culture and technology was based upon resins, saps, ambers, wood, and strange methods of sound. Even structures she'd have expected would use nails or cleverly-worked sticks were made with either some kind of paste or glue, or very interesting rope work. Eshkar's speech continued while she processed all of this. "But we do have our own kinds of Deep, usually when we get older. It can happen in fever, from head injuries, or love sickness."

She had to ask about that last one. They spent some back-and-forth on clarification before she realized that he meant diseases like syphilis. At first, the idea of love causing illness seemed off-putting, but she recalled that her own culture has written many songs driven by heartbreak or cynical takes on romance. All's fair. The fact that the dinos and the humans clearly had very different kinds of intelligence, but recognized and respected each other's minds and ways, was incredibly interesting to her.

She still had no idea how she was getting home. Nonetheless, she pressed the conversation on this Deepening phenomenon: "I take it that the different tribes of humans and dinos have different ideas about where the Deep comes from, and why it happens?"

He nodded. "It is why we must keep moving. Stillness might last for some time before there is any Deepening, but if we fall into it and we're not moving, it takes all the dinos, and the humans won't survive that. The dinos, for that matter, would either die from the chaos or...see to the matter once they've come back to their senses."

"But they can come back?"

He shifted his weight several times. Eshkar's expression had varied patches of tension and ticks, and he lulled his head back and forth. It seemed equal parts important and uncomfortable to him to talk about this. "Sort of. No one who has been in the Deep is the same after. Most of the time, the dinos feel great shame from it. Humans have tried to remind them that it's not their fault, but..."

"It's hard to shake the guilt," Cassidy finished for him.

"I get that." He frowned. "Where I'm from, life is plenty complicated, even without dinos and the Deep. Well, not the Deep like this, anyway. The humans I'm a part of can still have fevers and hurts and all the rest." Eshkar's chin slowly dipped and lifted again as he took this in. She was picturing everything she'd seen to this point: the (seeming?) violence of the dactyls, the triceratops when she'd crashed, the way they tried to stamp out this utuki and keep up their glow-trees, the stampede of stegoceras. "It seems like the utuki are never far off when the Deep is threatening," she mused to him. She still kept her voice low.

He looked at her like she was an idiot. "We try to wipe it out, it is bad for our amber toolery. But it is everywhere, and we are always moving. Besides, we smoke it. Wouldn't the smoke, or keeping samples of the flowers around, bring the Deep about right away?"

She scratched behind her ear. They were tingling from the sheer electric joy she was feeling to be in such an incredibly new situation. But she was also wrestling with many questions. "Are there always dactyls about when you find groves of the flower?"

"Not always," he said, "but often. And sometimes they come after us once we've set fire to the groves, if we're not quick enough in leaving."

"And the dactyls are violent, right?" she reasoned.

"They do not get the Deep," he said, with growing frustration. He struggled to keep that in check, and she could see that he was wrestling with his own questions. "Unless they are just always in the Deep."

"The common part here is the flowers," she pointed

out.

"But that's just as true of the trees, the soil, the air," he said. She had to acknowledge that his thinking made a kind of sense. Besides, if it were the flowers, that would raise an awful lot of questions — many of them intensely uncomfortable, given the smoking culture.

Cassidy phrased her thinking delicately. "Suppose the flowers only do this when they're still in the ground, alive and able to do their...usual thing?"

He looked around anxiously. The caravan was in full swing at this point. Medical platforms were organized and more populated than Cassidy would have liked. The Twin was on a different one than hers. Abnir was also elsewhere at this point, and the archaeologist couldn't find the leader among the crowd. Belessunu was part of the next platform over, and glanced Cassidy's way occasionally. She wondered if the dino wanted to talk more with her new human friend of the odd skin colour. Eshkar returned her to the conversation: "If that were true, it would explain why the smoking and keeping them in pouches makes no difference. But they are flowers. They have no magic for causing things around them."

"What about something like pheromones, pollen, or other signal systems?" she proposed.

"We have no words for what you're trying to say," he answered.

Interesting.

CHAPTER SEVEN

Cassidy looked around. "Do you have anything like magnifying glasses?"

"I don't understand the question. We use glass when we find it, usually for knives and other times when we need something sharp. The healers use it for surgery."

She'd noticed obsidian among their tools. Somewhat like the aztecs in that way, but not really; they still seemed to her like Babylonians or some other older Middle-Eastern civilization who didn't have metal and went down a very different road because of the resins and other unusual organic material here. "How do your scouts improve what they can see?" she asked.

"Some of our best healers have ways of making the eyes be the best they can be," he answered. "Why?"

"So you don't use glass for any tricks with light?" she pressed.

"Oh! That's what you've been getting at," he said. "Yes, we usually combine it with the amber toolery. Sometimes light levels are important for energy, and our builders have some interesting techniques. But what does this have to do with the Deep?"

"I have some ideas I want to try," she said. "Can you gather some of your friends for me? I'm looking for your tech— toolery, and research." He blinked at that. "Um," she tried again, "Your people who study. The ones who examine things, and come up with ideas for new toolery?"

"Ah, dreamers and believers," he said. "Belessunu leads some of them."

Human and dino science was shared. She supposed that made sense. "Please. I know I ask a lot, but if I could meet your idea leaders," she doubted they had a concept of science as she understood it, "then I might be able to help. I can add some of the things that my people know."

"I'll pass the message along now," he said, and he appeared to be oddly excited and relieved. "Abnir already speaks much about finding outside help for lasting problems, and I admit that I'm curious myself. So are many of the others. Now that things are settling down, it might not even take all that long. Until the march," and he set off.

Did that phrase mean goodbye?

"Thank you," she said as he set out. This left her some time to reflect. She had very serious doubts and concerns about sharing knowledge and technology. Her background in archaeology and anthropology addressed this concept many times. True, they were on the move and there were things about that which seemed pitiable to her. They didn't have any settled-down methods of study. They didn't seem to stop to smell the roses, including knowledge like pheromones, or signal systems like pollen. Though that could have been that he was a scout and not representative of all his people. She'd find that out soon enough.

But what about the risks of cultural interference? Did she have the right to meddle with their ways and beliefs just so she could get home? But if she didn't, she'd never get back! It wasn't like she could climb those trees, and even if she got above the canopy without falling or getting eaten by a pterodactyl, what was she to do? Jump to the portal? Not that she had much hope this way as it was. Even if she gave them new ways of dealing with this "Deep," it didn't help her climb out of her situation.

She'd have to adapt. She might be here for the rest of her life. It would be nice not to have to spend that time fending off random attacks. She also had to admit that she was fiercely curious. Not just about this amber technology — so many questions! — but also the dinos, the dactyls, and the whole environment. How high could the dactyls fly? What could she build, combining her knowledge with theirs? She wasn't in aviation, but everyone talks about lift and drag and all that at some point in high school or undergrad. Could she give them flight? Should she? If the dinos are people, just in bodies she usually associated with great beasts, why were the dactyls so wild and violent? Was this a cultural divide? Did she have the right or ability to bridge that divide?

She was left to her own devices for longer than she'd have liked. Minor activities blurred the day: dashes, swings, and dives of the scouts among the enormous trees; bursts of discussion and odd glances among the deinocheirus; shifts in the positions of the platforms; many of the running and jumping dinos coming and going. She couldn't help but note the greatly reduced numbers of compsognathus after those scuttling dinos turned or fell during the Deepening of the stegoceras.

None of the influential people she'd spoken to — like Abnir or the Twin — came back her way.

An escort of scouts landed all about her. They moved with such acrobatic grace that even watching one of them coming for her still felt like it came out of nowhere. Their movements were hard to predict. She doubted this was accidental. "They've decided to hear you," one of the scouts said.

"Wonderful," Cassidy replied. "How do I...?" One of them bent in a gesture she knew from her own culture: piggyback riding. "Oh," she said, and climbed on the other woman's back. At first, she felt somewhat insulted, but it didn't last: dismounting a large dino was one thing, but she could never have kept up with the swinging, gliding, and ropework that these people were accomplishing. Before she knew it, she was up in the trees.

The caravan was stopping. Platforms were lowered and unstrapped from the deinocheirus, and they were afforded the opportunity to rest. With punctuated brevity, the group disembarked and unmounted their people and supplies, the dinos shifting in their conversations and responsibilities. Meshed and lashed branches and fibres; all manner of wooden components; some resinous structures and tools whose purposes were less obvious; bridges, shelters, and rope wizardry; all quickly turned the patch of treebound and hole-pocked ground into an ad hoc village.

There were no circles of fire this time. She was tossed about as the scouts did their work, and didn't actually realize right away that she was on her own feet on the ground again. "What's going on?" she asked some nearby oviraptors who were performing minor errands.

"Heartwood Council," one of them said. "That's where you'll come in."

One of its fellows added, pointing with her tail, "Over yonder, you'll be in that amber circle. Big rumble, this. Not a lot of councils."

"Ah. Well, thank you."

"Don't mention it."

Before long, the intelligentsia of the tribe were collected with her inside a circle of sap technologies she didn't recognize and some wood-and-amber guns whose purpose was clearer. They were all aimed up, toward the canopy. A slow rotation of dino guards roved outside the circle.

"Many of us think you might be a threat," said an oviraptor who clearly held some position of command. The council was one quarter human and the other three quarters were different varieties of dino: small runners like the oviraptor, armoured ones like an ankylosaurus, and bulkier ones including a tyrannosaurus. The latter was far from the biggest dino of the tribe, but probably the largest they could manage for keeping in a meeting. Of course, there was no guarantee that size was the actual guiding principle here.

"Others believe you are an adorable curiosity, but no help to us," said one of the armoured dinos. "We've survived thus far, and shall continue."

"Still others," Abnir said pointedly, "have more hope than that."

The tyrannosaurus said, "It is time we heard your plans, u-halbu. We will help you and answer what questions we can, and we are confident you will contribute to us fairly." This one was so calm that Cassidy had to remind herself that the movies got a little excited about their predators.

Cassidy tapped her chin. "I am glad to have met you all," she began carefully, "and have learned much. But I didn't come here to visit. I was just doing a fly-by." To their various glances and mutterings she answered, "I was taking in some of the sights, getting a sense for what's around. It was supposed to be quicker than this. I'm probably missed back home."

"So you wish to return," Abnir surmised. She remained stiff-backed and proud, but Cassidy thought she caught a note of disappointment.

"Not without giving you all my gratitude," Cassidy quickly clarified, "but yes." She thought it just as well to start from the beginning. Not quite from the dig in Iran where Gamgee had located the portal. Nor after that, when they found a deep cavern and a wall that had clearly been built with great effort to withstand the test of time. Certainly not when the team drilled through the wall into — impossibly — the sky. She skipped the part about being supplied a Cessna as well. "I have to fly to get back home. It would take too long to explain why. But I think I can help you. I believe the dactyls have intelligence. They might even be people."

Outrage. Grumbling, yelling, argument.

A dino with a longer neck, not actively part of the council, let out a shriek that could have sent the sap back into the trees. This was a magyarosaurus: much smaller than the well-known brontosaurus, it had some bony armour on its back but otherwise bore out the comparison. This one appeared to be a moderator or facilitator of some kind. Grudgingly, the various leaders collected themselves. The oviraptor said, "What you say is heresy. Gliding is sometimes necessary, but true flight is evil — that is why some of us distrust you. More than that, dactyls are violent, chaotic, and merciless. They are no more people than a landslide. And they come — many sing it — from the Ear."

"What's the Ear?" Cassidy had to ask.

"A hole in the sky," answered the magyarosaurus. "We can tell little about it from so far below it, but it always stays above the Temple of Hearkening. You must have seen it, if you were flying?"

She'd come from it. "Yes, I have — and thank you," she answered the moderator. She turned back to the oviraptor. "And I believe the dactyls showed tactics and intelligence when we fought them last, by the mushrooms," Cassidy pressed.

"Only we had tactics," said the ankylosaurus spokesperson.

This was the problem, Cassidy reflected, with always being on — always on the move, always rushing, always pushing the grind. You never stopped to look at things another way. As an adrenaline junkie, she struggled with it herself. She addressed the armoured ones: "They went for the amber weapons," she started.

"Hardly conclusive," the tyrannosaurus cut in. "If something were striking even an animal, they'd run or they'd attack it back, right?"

"A fair point," she had to acknowledge, "but it doesn't stop there. They didn't really come in much other than to go for those weapons — yes, I know, but let me finish. They plucked humans up, didn't they?"

"They eat us," Abnir said, "and they've long done so. You are not from the forest, it seems, so you wouldn't know that there's little food to be had up there."

"Has anyone been up there to see what they eat?" Cassidy asked the entire group.

They radiated pride. They were angry, insulted. But they looked at one another. "It is known…" the oviraptor started.

"Common sense is dangerous," Cassidy warned. "I'm sure you have your climbers," she softened, "and your explorers and the like." Numerous nods. "I saw an awful lot of those dactyls up above the forest, before my plane was wrecked," she pointed out. "So, how is it that they don't hunt you more? Why are they always around utuki when they do attack you, and why didn't they keep after you once we backed off?"

"Too dangerous."

"They're not that bright."

"There are many humans, not just our tribe."

"Some sing that dactyls eat each other."

"Who is this u-halbu to spill her thinking all over us like mushroom flow?"

"I thought we were here about the utuki."

"If you know so much, go talk to them."

"I plan to," Cassidy Cane said to the ankylosaurus.

Their hubbub came to an abrupt halt. They stared at

her incredulously.

"You can't be serious," Abnir said.

Humans, it seemed, were wonderfully different every-where — and yet always human. Cassidy wondered, not for the first or last time, how these dinosaurs could look even remotely similar to the ones she knew of from her world. The brain power for true intelligence, and the ability to speak, would surely have led to seriously obvious differences in their bodies. But that was beside the point.

"I can and I am. I think the dactyls cherry-picked their targets, and that they do the people-eating thing as a scare tactic," said the archaeologist from another world.

The human leader responded, "It certainly works!"

Unbelievably, this garnered general amusement through little sniffs, snorts, and dino gestures that Cassidy was learning were the equivalent of a chuckle. They used body language somewhat differently than humans did, but that made sense: they weren't the same as the humans. Cassidy flashed Abnir a glimpse of gratitude.

"We have often witnessed dactyls and utuki together," the oviraptor remarked, "but they are both evil. It is to be expected."

"You must hope to reach the dactyls through the utuki, then?" asked the tyrannosaur.

"Just so," Cassidy confirmed.

"Dino religion forbids it," said the ankylosaurus. "The glow-trees, sown from the holy seeds of knowledge, must be protected. The utuki, destroyed. There could be no communion with it in any case — it is a plant."

Cassidy was sorely tempted to ask about human religion, how they could be different but alongside one another, and if it really came down to one species with one religion and all the dino species grouped together with the other. It was one thing for humans to be united, but such a union of belief between many species? How? She'd pressed the boundaries of her luck and their faith already, asking about the Deep and challenging their views. She hadn't thrilled like this in years, but her head worked at any heartbeat except zero.

"I do not ask you to go beyond your beliefs," she said. "But it seems clear to me — regardless of the specifics — that there's more to these dactyls and the flowers than the knowledge you can share with me. That much, at least, we can agree on."

"In a basic way, yes," Abnir conceded. The dino representatives each nodded as she continued. "But while our beliefs do not hinder us from going with you as humans, we must show solidarity to our dino brethren. And we cannot bear the brunt of another assault like the last one without dino support." Again, the other leaders nodded their agreement with the human.

"I wouldn't ask you to," Cassidy said. "And I'm sure it would be great to live my days out with both your kinds."

"But you would not be home," the ankylosaurus said. Whatever differences the armoured ones might have with her, it seemed they weren't completely without empathy or understanding.

It was Cassidy's turn to nod.

"What then?" asked the tyrannosaurus.

"Lend me a way of covering some real distance," she said, "and perhaps a small amount of supplies or instructions from the humans so I can get by. Send me forward with as small a group as possible — say, one dino who could get me there quickly."

"Where did you have in mind?" the oviraptor folded his claws over one another, curving out his feathered arms.

"Wherever we can find another patch of the flower," Cassidy answered.

"Too dangerous," the armoured ones objected immediately.

"Only to me, really," Cassidy said, then corrected herself, "...and the dino who brings me there. The scouts who find it are only to locate the grove and return, so they shouldn't even be noticed."

"You ask much," the tyrannosaurus remarked.

"But not too much," Cassidy agreed. "It's not just for myself, you see: I could bring back knowledge."

"Some might think you are trying to change our way of life," Abnir remarked. Hers was not a tone of approval.

"How you live is up to you," Cassidy replied carefully. "But it sounds like this quest of yours to stamp out the flower has been going on for an awfully long time. You have so many risks," and she was about to mention what the Deep could do them if it happened too much, too quickly, at the wrong time. Looking at three-quarters of the representatives of the council, though, she saw dinos. Only dinos were affected so immediately and violently. Such a remark would have cost her dearly. "...And so much to be gained. Just let me get close enough to the grove that I could walk to it in reasonable time. Say, half an hour off. Then the dino who brought be that far — and the scouts who might be watching — can back away as far and safely as they wish. I suggest completely."

"Why?" the oviraptor asked. "Do you not think our peoples brave?"

"On the contrary!" she replied. "You've all proven your bravery. But if the dactyls are there and they notice I'm not alone, they might rally their attack — or defence. If it's just me…"

"…they might stop enough to be curious," the tyrannosaurus finished for her.

She nodded. The ankylosaurus said, "We admire your courage in venturing to go alone, and your care for not putting our people at needless risk."

"I believe we can adjourn here," Abnir said. The dinos nodded as she continued, "The Heartwood Council will speak among ourselves now, u-halbu, and we invite you to rest or spend time with our peoples as you choose. You will be informed what we decide."

Cassidy was a little taken aback, as she'd hoped to arrive at the decision together. "Thank you," was all that she could manage as she did her best to walk away with dignity. The yelling started practically the moment her feet landed on soil outside of their circle. She caught something like "another tribe would be better" and something about the importance of belief. Variants of "leader" and "leadership" were bandied about, but she did her best to be out of hearing. It would be all too easy for some scout she couldn't see to report later that she'd been eavesdropping.

This much she knew: there were divisive politics at

play, and she had supporters. It would have to do. Eshkar
was waiting for her once she was closer to the common
community. "You made it," he joked.

She lifted a dimple. "So did you."

"Come with me," he said, and he did not wait for her
but turned and strode along. He kept talking with the ex-
pectation that she'd be there to hear him. "The Twin and
Belessunu were hoping to work with you."

She was pleasantly surprised. "Oh? On what?"

"I'd like to join you. We were thinking we could talk
toolery for a while."

It took two hours for the council to bring her their ver-
dict. In that time, she had some fun with her three unusual new friends. She showed them a magnifying glass
she had among her personal effects. They talked about
other tools and techniques as well, but that one stood out
to them because they thought all glass was black. Most of
their stuff, if it were not rope or wood, used lacquering
techniques with various resins and gums to create wondrous properties in the rope, wood, or glass — and to just
have the amber as its own thing.

Some additional scouts showed up when the decision
was reached. "We're to find a grove," they told Eshkar.

"Until the march," he said in farewell, and immediately set about his duties. Cassidy was having trouble
with the abruptness of these people, but it made a kind of
sense: if you had to keep moving to survive, you'd have a
no-nonsense attitude.

The scouts turned to her. "You're to rest and prepare.
Some of us will be detailed for your supply, instruction,
and guidance."

"What instruction?" she asked.

"You improvised well, and it does you credit," another of them responded. "But there's a proper technique for moving with dinos. We will show you the ropes. We expect that everything will be in step for the morning."

And so it was.

Their operation was prompt, communication was clear and efficient, and she was bouncing along on the back of Mashda the corythosaurus in no time. Her breakfast had been something a lot like honey: they doled it out in little bulbs, and you ate the thing whole. "It'll give you your day's energy and strength for muscle and bone," the Twin had explained to her, "but you can't live off the stuff by itself for long."

"Thank you," she'd said a thousand times, and bid her farewells.

CHAPTER EIGHT

Now roots larger than some buildings she'd seen in her day were zipping by her on either side. The ground seemed to vary in contour, thickness of soil, and so on — but Mashda had no trouble keeping her comfortable and on-track. There were vibrato clicking sounds from high up in the trees every once in a while. By now she'd learned to look for them: they weren't lizards or birds, but scouts using special wooden whistles for signalling while still sounding like wildlife.

Eventually, there was just one sound, and it was high-pitched and drawn-out. The casual observer might have thought it was a lizard declaring its presence to rivals or potential mates. But the corythosaurus stopped, allowed Cassidy to get down, and turned. "May your path be generous," she said.

"And yours," Cassidy said. Her mount looked at her funny, and she was reminded of awkward moments like telling the waiter to also enjoy their meal. Mashda left. Cassidy, now accustomed to the ways of the scouts, occasionally caught small glimpses of them leaping or swinging amidst the branches.

Resisting the temptation to wave — which might give them away to unwanted viewers — Cassidy turned forward. She couldn't quite make out the grove from here, but trusted that the directions she'd been given were accurate. Huffing once, she set out.

It took closer to forty-five minutes, not half an hour, for her to reach the grove. She doubted they'd misjudged the distance. Two dactyls were among the flowers. They hadn't noticed her yet. She took the risk to look up, and had to crane her neck and look hard. But there were more up there. A shadow here, a reptilian caw there. She brought her gaze to bear on the two in the grove, clasped her hands in front of her in plain view, and waited.

They noticed her.

Their shock was unmistakable. They weren't making as many sounds as she'd expected. They looked at each other, then took stock of the plants. She made it a point to show them that she was keeping her distance from the utuki. Broken branches, leaves, fruits, and other bits of detritus fell in a gentle alarm. She didn't bother to look up — winning a fight wasn't an option anyway.

One of the dactyls made its way over. The other watched intently. Cassidy didn't know what to make of that. She allowed the one before her to give her a thorough examination. Its method of walking was peculiar. They had two legs and two wings, whose patagium connected at the leg and not the backs or sides. The wings were so much larger than, well, all of it, that the dactyl used the long edges as a sort of large makeshift foot. Now that she was watching closely, the archaeologist realized that the flowers were growing in an arrangement. Possibly not a true pattern, but it was awfully coincidental that there was always an opportunity for the dactyl to put down a wing in order to walk about.

Which worked well enough — she doubted wings of that size could beat without causing harm to the plants. But why would it care? While she pondered this and examined the dactyl's body, it sniffed at her, stared head to toe, and made throat and mouth movements she couldn't decipher. Eventually, the dactyl made so far as to poke and bump at her.

"Whoa!" she said as she fell.

The dactyl glanced at the flowers at its side, just to be sure. Once she'd stood up and collected herself, with the dactyl watching her warily, she realized it hadn't meant to knock her down — and didn't intend to take another risk yet.

"Cassidy," she said, pointing at herself. "Cass-ih-dee."

The moment she made sound, its eyes narrowed and it tilted its head toward her. It moved its mouth, similar to before, and she could see micro-muscle vibrations running along its upper chest and throat in parallel lines. She pantomimed listening, and faced different directions, trying to show that she wasn't getting it.

The dactyl made two more attempts before Cassidy heard a sound coming from its throat that was somewhere between an avian reptile cry and a large plumping dollop of water. Cassidy's eyes widened and she pointed at the creature. Both dactyls responded with an excited exchange between them that just looked to Cassidy like vibrating at each other.

So they used sound beyond human ears. Or at least, beyond hers. Could the tribespeople hear them, she wondered?

"Cassidy," she said again.

The human and the dactyl made several more attempts. "Hm," she mused. "It doesn't look like this is going to work." She looked around and picked up a stick, then she gestured with it. "Come along," and she headed for a flatter and more accessible stretch of soil.

The dactyl made a sound that was at first a confused kind of surprise, but it did follow when it realized she wasn't coming back to it — or the grove. Its colleague? Partner? She didn't even know how to tell their sexes apart. The other one approached the nearer end of the grove, but did not go beyond. It reminded Cassidy of a sentinel.

She had roughly twenty-four hours before the scouts or a dino would come back to the same spot to see if they could retrieve her. The fact that the dactyls hadn't already eaten her was a good sign that her hunch was at least partly accurate. She began drawing in the dirt. She started with a little stick figure for herself, pointed at herself, and said, "Cassidy."

The dactyl watched. There was a gleam in its eyes. Oddly, she was reminded of Gamgee. She didn't know how that made her feel. Shrugging that off, she focused on how to proceed. She had to avoid confusion. Drawing a group of stick figures, she pointed away and said, "Humans."

The dactyl kept its chin lifted and lowered its head forward before lifting again, as though drawing the bottom half of a circle in the air. It was nothing like a nod. Did it have the same meaning as one, or was the dactyl as out of its depth as she felt?

She tried a few more: a tree, and she pointed at one; she avoided the flowers, but drew and pointed at a near-by shrub-like plant; a rock; the dactyls. She had to keep moving along the ground, and in some cases skipped over little pits or patches of plants, in order to continue using fresh ground. She was worried the act of erasing an image would convey an unintended message. If she erased a dactyl image, would they take that as a threat?

For the time being, it watched. Occasionally the dactyl would perform one of its wing-steps between the different groupings of drawings, bending and turning its head sidelong so it could get a good look at the ground. Her strides were much shorter than the dactyl's, so she had to put in much more work to cover the same space. It seemed to be looking at each drawing separately, then taking them in as a whole. While Cassidy pondered how to proceed, the dactyl abruptly approached a patch of soil and used a wing's broadside to brush an area clean. It was careful to restore the soil to the original position so that it would still have something to write upon. It assiduously avoided disturbing plants, and stopped whenever rabbits or similar critters went to and fro.

It then re-drew some of the images Cassidy had made.

It made one of itself, pointing to itself with the little outcropping of fingers at the topside tip of one wing. It used the pointed end of its wing as a large finger for the soil-drawing. It made another, slightly smaller dactyl, and pointed at its friend — which was indeed smaller than itself. Then it drew three dactyls, hastily and with less detail, and pointed to both itself and its cohort. While the human took this in, it proceeded to imitate the images Cassidy had made of herself and the humans, pointing to the group of three stick men and the three dactyls.

Cassidy couldn't believe what she was seeing. The dactyl was clearly working with her to develop what amounted to a primitive writing system! It was intelligent! But it didn't seem to have any way to easily interface with her outside of this method. Small wonder there was no talk between them and the tribes!

But the way the archaeologist understood things, these groups had been in conflict for a span at least as long as multiple generations. Possibly even into their equivalent of antiquity. If it could pick up on writing this easily, why hadn't dactyls as a whole found a way to get through to the tribes?

Excited and curious, the two began a lengthy process of developing simple methods of expressing things to each other.

She decided to try again. "Cassidy," she said, pointing at herself.

The dactyl regarded her without response.

She reflected and drew a more elaborate person in the soil, emphasizing some of her articles of clothing — like pilot goggles and her leather jacket — instead of the furs and woven plants worn by the humans of the tribe. Then she drew a few extra stick people, circled her image, and pointed again at herself. "Cassidy."

CHAPTER NINE

The dactyl's throat and chest produced vibrations along lines that she could see now that she was closer. It didn't make any sounds that she could detect, though. Then it brushed out the space again and drew two dactyls, one larger than the other. It stopped, looked around this way and that, and sat with a pensive, far-off look in its eyes. Then it drew on the larger dactyl image an imitation of the jagged scar it had on its leg. It made two or three flowers under the feet of the smaller one — which had yet to leave the circle of the utuki.

Cassidy clapped her hands in delight. They understood individual identity and were responding to her attempts! Clearly they saw that she was trying to identify herself to them. She reflected upon the situation. "I'm going to call you Albatross," she said to the one with which she'd been conversing. "Either I win your favour and sail home, or I bring you harm and you doom me. Seems fitting," she remarked with a nervous chuckle.

Albatross, after previously only watching her, this time leaned its head toward her. It had turned to face its ear at her.

"Can you not hear me?"

Turned this way, it couldn't really look at her. She took this as a sign of trust. But it didn't respond when she spoke.

"Oh," she said with a mixture of disappointment and accomplishment. That would go a long way to explaining why human, dino, and dactyl weren't talking — they seemed to use a different sound range!

She decided to call the one in the flowers Roc, to stay on the theme of birds in myth. She didn't bother telling them — that was too advanced for stick men, and they couldn't hear her anyway. She did, however, point at Roc and draw out a hasty set of the two dactyls and herself, with some scratched out utuki to the side. She even drew an arrow starting from the plants and going to the picture of Roc.

Albatross thumped down its wing tip on the picture of Roc and circled the flowers.

Cassidy scrunched up her face, standing back to let Albatross clear the turf and explain itself. It drew Roc in detailed caricature, enlarging the head enough that it could draw a brain inside Roc's picture. It then drew a detailed image of the utuki. Cassidy was surprised by the specifics. The dactyls were so large that she wouldn't have expected them to be able to get down enough to get a good look at the plants. These plants were large to her — not counting the stem, the plant would take up a five-gallon jug — but next to the dactyls?

She held up an index finger, hoping the sign for "hold on a sec" would make the leap over their cultural divide, and carefully made her way over to the grove. Albatross immediately made a single warning bark-like sound. It was too reptilian to be like a household pet, but the sound came with the same biting motion of a snout and it was short and punctuating. Cassidy got down on all fours, well before the plants, and gently made her way closer, exaggerating her investigation in the hopes that they would realize that she was just looking.

Roc was not impressed and made its way over to the human with delicate but precise haste. Its jaw snapped within inches of Cassidy and she backed off. Collecting herself, Cassidy returned to the drawing patch, satisfied that she'd seen enough to recognize that in fact Albatross' pictures were accurate. To her surprise, it hadn't continued drawing, and was watching her now with a combination of worry and consternation.

"Yeah, you warned me," she had to acknowledge. She pointed to the image and watched as Albatross resumed. It tapped near the picture of Roc's brain, careful not to disturb the scratches in the soil, and tapped spots in the soil over the flower, gesturing back and forth between what looked like pollen and Roc's brain.

Are the flowers good for their brains? But they're not eating the utuki. "Are you saying that they're enhancing your mind somehow?" she asked aloud, and remembered that wouldn't go far. Was utuki a kind of pterodactyl peyote? Was Albatross being metaphorical?

She drew a stick man, a picture of the fruits on a nearby bush (pointing as she went), and drew an arrow from the fruit through the mouth of the stick man and pointing at the stomach. She then used her stick to point to the picture of the utuki and the one of Roc, imitating eating as she did.

Albatross hopped side to side, making several distressed half-flaps of its wings and snapping its jaws in consternation. It circled the stomach area of Roc and then X'd it out. It then looked at its compatriot in the grove and they exchanged a bunch of vibrations which were silent to the human, but clearly intense.

With anger, it wiped the whole thing and started again, drawing with such aggression now that dirt flew. A stick man, large and a little silly, with a detailed tube and fire at the end. Utuki with a fire over it. Several different varieties of dino, all with arrows pointing to a picture of an X'd out brain. An elaborate human head with more teeth than necessary, angry-pointed eyes, an X'd out brain in the head, and a line going from the burning flower to two pictures of brains in the human's chest.

Then it redrew the stick man with goggles — Cassidy — and put a brain in the head, making oval circles where it expected lungs to be.

She moved back and forth between the pictures, having to walk for a span in several cases because this was taking significant space (and time, for that matter — daylight wouldn't last much longer), and worked out what Albatross was trying to say. As far as she could tell, it was vehemently opposed to smoking (or perhaps just smoking that particular plant) and it seemed to think that the tribespeople (both human and dino) were brainless beasts or monsters. She, it seemed, was an exception to the dactyl.

Fascinating!

She pantomimed wiping up the images, and the dactyl

obliged. She tapped her chin, thinking about what to do next, and felt she had to make a concession. While she'd been getting used to the dimness of the forest, it was getting late. She pointed at her eyes, and spread out her arms, then pointed up and cupped her hands at the wrists to make the shape of a half-sun.

Albatross glanced at the grove, hop-skipped a little farther away to be safe, and burst into the air. She craned her neck, but lost sight of it amid the branches before it even reached the canopy. She regarded Roc, who was content to furrow amid the flowers and who glanced up at the human only to make an odd shuffling gesture and return to its...work? Play? Something else?

Suddenly illumination spilled about them. Albatross had returned with a bundle of what looked like bioluminescent slugs. They were as large as black bears, and inched along without a care in the world once they were set aright on the ground. Albatross pointed at the drawing patch and sat back, intent.

Well, then.

She set about elaborately drawing counter-points to some of what the dactyl had expressed, eventually getting across that the dinos and other humans do in fact have brains. This seemed to disturb, offend, or irritate Albatross in some way, but it made no move to stop her. She reflected for a second, and decided to take the risk of her hunch.

She drew an utuki, a brain, and X'd out the brain, using an arrow to make sure her message was clear.

The dactyl didn't stomp with its (relatively) tiny feet, but with the sides of its wings. It snapped at Cassidy so hard that she couldn't believe it didn't break its own teeth, and she was knocked back onto her rear by the sheer force of the snap. She also got more breath than she could ever have wanted to smell in her life, and concluded that mint was not among the plants here — or that dactyls must not have liked it.

Albatross cleared the patch and angrily drew a robust image of the utuki. To the side, it drew a large and detailed brain-like shape, but made it in segments like a jigsaw puzzle. It then drew a whole brain inside the pistil, rendering arrows from that through the stamens and into the air. At the end of each arrow, it drew individual jigsaw pieces of the brain.

Cassidy stared in disbelief. "You're saying the plants are people? They can think?"

Albatross bumped its own jaw with the nearby point of its wing, as though punching itself in the mouth, and pointed fervently at the drawing patch.

"Right," she muttered to herself.

They spent the remainder of the evening in the light of the slug-things, repeating and counter-pointing their drawings until each was certain the other understood.

Dactyls had a relationship with the plants not unlike human and dino. Utuki could think and communicate, at least in some fashion, and — as far as Cassidy could make out — the dactyls were defending them in what they saw as a genocidal war! That seemed a little out of her pay grade.

In the morning, Cassidy awoke to find that several additional dactyls (all adults) had joined them. Roc was associating with the others and two different dactyls were now attending, or communing with, the grove. Roc broke off from the others to deliver to Cassidy some objects that had been conveyed by a dactyl who dropped them off and left again. It was a bundle of edible things such as mushrooms, fruits, a nut-like thing, and — to her surprise — a cooked rabbit. She glanced around and could find no sign of any fire. Had they cooked it for her elsewhere? Did they cook their own food? If not, she didn't know if she could trust the meat. She cut into it with one of her knives and found that it had been cooked through.

"All in," she said to herself, and surprised herself with her own gusto.

Being a diplomat for dinosaurs and dactyls was hungry work.

Well, diplomat was excessive, but she didn't know what else to think of it.

Once she was done, she joined them at the drawing patch and noticed that there were bones piled up in the nook of a tree where Albatross had been feeding. She decided not to look at those bones too closely. It seems they'd all been waiting on her, and Albatross approached. It turned sidelong and dropped so that the upper side of its half-stretched wing was exposed to her. The others watched.

"Um, thanks?" she asked, knowing she wouldn't get a response, and decided to imitate its motions. She didn't have an equivalent of wings, but the way she positioned herself effectively exposed her back to it. Satisfied, Albatross stood and resumed its place opposite the sizeable span of flat soil the pair had been using to communicate. The others afforded their comrade and the odd human some room. When Cassidy stood and gazed at them all, she got the vague impression that they approved.

Wasting no more time, Cassidy set about expressing the concept of the — from their perspective — earth in the sky. She had to know if they could get her home.

As part of the back-and-forth, she indicated the canopy and the portal she used. She then drew differing heights of dactyl flight. There was some confusion until she tried a different approach: stepping back, she jumped on the spot — which felt ridiculous, surrounded as she was by giant predatory reptilian flyers. She then drew a stick man with her trademark goggles, and used that next to the picture of a tree to indicate her jump height. She flapped her arms and pointed at all of them and then back to the pictures.

Several exchanges later, she was confident she understood: they could make it to the portal, but it was very high, and took so much effort that they generally only used it for...fighting? Punishment? Maybe something like the game Tag? Albatross' friends, or family, or — for all she knew — co-workers all seemed to be tickled pink by this whole exercise. Sometimes they played, sometimes they did other things that she felt she shouldn't watch.

She was wrestling with how to proceed when Albatross took up the lead. It started with the portal and used lightning bolts and arrows with rocks to indicate explosion or bursting through. It added an image of her Cessna. "So you know that was me, huh?" she asked aloud. If it noticed her talk, it gave no sign. It went on with X'd out pictures of dactyls.

She wasn't having any of that.

"You attacked me!" she said as she went to work establishing the fault.

The process stopped. Albatross snapped its head up and regarded Cassidy for a long instant. She stood up straight and matched its gaze. If it attacked, she had no chance. She didn't care. They'd have to respect her and take her seriously if she was going to get anywhere here. "I wasn't out to hurt anyone. Your deaths are on you," she said.

A predatory lean — heard and felt more than seen — loomed over her from her audience.

Eventually, her dactyl counterpart took up the conversation once more.

Erasing the images so far, it drew itself carrying stick-Cassidy on its back to the portal. Then it drew a simplified image of one of the platforms the tribes suspended from the backs of the deinocheirus, which had become their symbol for a tribe. It made a stick-picture of an utuki with wings -- the symbol for the dactyl version of a tribe. And it made a harsh, jagged line separating the two.

If she was reading this right, Albatross was offering her a deal: I'll get you home if you'll make them leave the flowers alone.

It took a significant amount of drawing before Cassidy was confident that the message was clear: she was going to show the tribe the system she'd worked out with the dactyls and start a dialogue. She hoped her new dactyl friend — at least, not-an-enemy — understood that she wasn't making any promises. She considered indicating that she might return in the future, but thought better of it. Whether she did or not, that should be at a time and for a reason of her choosing.

A new, smaller dactyl arrived and there was a flurry of activity and, uh, chest-vibrating. Albatross was the only one who seemed terribly concerned about how Cassidy fit into this. It drew for her a dactyl-tribe, a curved line at its edge like a border, and a platform-tribe just outside that line.

She drew herself on the line.

Albatross met her eyes again. This time there was no obvious hostility, and she thought she saw something like affection or approval. Albatross turned, did some of that throbbing they do, and the smallest dactyl flew down in front of Cassidy. She couldn't help but remember the scout who'd bent for her to do a piggyback ride, because the body language was remarkably similar. She swallowed nervously.

Time for a test flight!

CHAPTER TEN

Once they arrived at the meeting place, Cassidy was overjoyed to get off the beast. It was like being in a bouncy castle if the balloons were somehow as hard as wood. She hurt everywhere, and would probably show a legion of bruises by tomorrow. In the dactyl's defence, they weren't used to carrying people, and clearly thought it would be easier than it was.

She was much too jostled to notice any scouts in the trees. Before her was Mashda. "It's not as bad as it looks!" she called out as she got off the dactyl in an undignified scramble. She turned to her former carrier. "Thank you," she said, knowing it wouldn't understand her words, but hoping it grasped her expression.

It examined her with some dismay, but made no effort to draw on the ground. First it crouched into an odd huddle, which she got the impression was directed at her, then it backed away two steps before turning and taking to the air again. She tried to remember that there could be cultural mistranslation happening here, but her gut feeling was that it felt guilty for giving her such a rough ride. She'd noticed along the way that it did what it could to glide, which made things smoother, but that brought the dactyl lower to the ground than was comfortable.

The corythosaurus watched it fly away with unsuppressed relief and a tinge of disgust. When it turned its attention to the human, she was already in the process of climbing up the rope on the side that was cleverly aligned along the body and beside the leg, making trips and snags less likely. She was perfectly happy not letting the dino get a good look at her. "Did they mistreat you?" she asked Cassidy as she headed them both back to the tribe.

"No," Cassidy said, "they were suspicious at first and half-tempted to just eat me. I have news for the tribe. We should all talk together."

She spent the day explaining what had happened and trying to get them to agree to learn the primitive writing system she'd worked out with the dactyls as a starting point. She was shocked by how much argument that took: they couldn't get past the idea that the dactyls weren't monsters. When she talked about the utuki possibly having some kind of intelligence or relationship with intelligent beings, they sent her off to the Twin and wouldn't hear anything more until he cleared her as physically and mentally sound. Four of the humans' experts on the ways of the mind — somewhat like shamans, as far as she could make it — examined her at length after that.

The following day, Cassidy was again before the Heartwood Council. Eshkar and Belessunu were also in attendance, along with the Twin and Mashda. Several hours of debate and explanation ensued. After a break for physical and mental refreshment, they resumed.

"We never were clear on why flight is so important for

your return home," Abnir said. She rubbed her bandaged leg as she sat. It was improving, but she'd need at least another week before she was in top-shape.

Cassidy had already made her needs clear to the dactyls. If she kept that from the tribespeople now, things could go poorly. "There's a mountain," she started, "though I can't even point to it now because I'd have to be above the canopy. I'm hopelessly turned about. It looks like the mountain used to be some kind of fortress, and the whole top of it is worked. Above it..."

"The Temple of Hearkening," said the tyrannosaurus, representative of the larger dinos. "Above it, the Ear."

Cassidy swallowed. This was going to be awkward. "I...um...do you remember how I explained that my wings, made of stuff called metal that you don't have, brought me to these lands?" They all nodded. "I flew it here from that cave in the sky. I'm from the Ear."

She expected uproar, hostility, a hubbub of commentary.

Instead, everyone present stared at her in stupefied silence.

"I don't have any way to repair my plane," she said. "Only the dactyls can fly. They're my only way home."

"It is sung that the dactyls come from the Ear," the ankylosaurus responded. "The Temple of Hearkening was re-fashioned by ancient humans while they strove to beat back the dactyl menace. You say there are humans, and no dactyls, where you are from?"

"Well, there are fossils," she corrected. "Ancient bones, of dactyl and dino alike, which we know to be hundreds of millions of years old because of our sciences. Our studies and toolery, as you put it."

"That...that doesn't make sense," the oviraptor said. Several others nodded.

"Our new human friend may be odd, but she has never steered us falsely and often helped us," Belessunu said.

Thank you, Cassidy mouthed as the deinocheirus nodded her support.

"I don't know what we expected," Eshkar said, "when we took a toss of the bones and chanced on the help of u-halbu. The forest has always been the forest. The forest is the world and the world is the forest. The trees are the mountains are the trees. So it is sung."

"So it is sung," echoed many of those in attendance.

"You rode to them," the armoured one mused, "and rode back. Alive. That alone is a worthy feat." He looked at the corythosaurus. "What can you tell us?"

"Not much," Mashda replied somewhat bashfully. "I carried Cassidy, and there were dactyls watching and wary. But they did not attack, I think, because she was right — so few, so cautious, and so far from the utuki, we clearly weren't there for violence. When I came back for her, she was shaken up, but she says this was from the dactyl's lack of carrying skill."

"Is this true?" Abnir asked of Cassidy.

"It is," she confirmed, "and I do not blame them. Your whole way of life includes having dinos help humans cover large distances. Dactyls only have the flowers, and I think they tend to and protect them."

"That much, at least, we seem to agree upon," said the tyrannosaurus. "Have you anything else to add?" he asked the corythosaurus.

"Only this: there was one dactyl, and no more. It seemed to consider Cassidy's well-being important, and made sure she was of sound health before leaving. I did not like to see our u-halbu so shaken, but I cannot deny my eyes — the dactyls did not attack, and I believe her words," she replied.

"I have made my desires clear," Cassidy said, "and my concerns. I assume you take me at my word that they can get me home, and that I need to return. But will you do as I asked?"

"A dialogue with them, and treating the utuki as anything other than a menace, is asking much," the ankylosaurus said. "Far too dangerous."

"But we do not have to come at it all at once," answered the oviraptor. The other dinos looked at him in surprise.

"I, for one, am curious about this writing you spoke of," Abnir said, "though I do not share your hope for what a conversation might accomplish. If all of this is as you say, and they are people, we may still have to fight. What they are harms us, and we have done them much hurt."

"Of course," Cassidy replied. "I don't expect you all to become instant friends. But it's worth a try. And if my guess is right, the flowers are causing the Deep."

"Yet you expect us not to be all the more motivated to wipe them out," said the tyrannosaurus.

"What if they're just defending themselves? Or even trying to communicate?" Cassidy said.

"Again, that is a lot," the oviraptor remarked. "But I have to agree on this: if you must fly above the Temple of Hearkening, only the dactyls can do that. We could offer you no help or protection, even if we wanted to."

"I would like to take some of your toolery — something simple, not too important — for my people to study at home," Cassidy said.

"We see no harm in this," Abnir said. "But it has to be something you can carry; we will not send our people amidst such dangers to carry gifts for you."

"That's fair," Cassidy said. "And I will try to return, perhaps with aid of some kind."

"Would it not be best to have you here for any talk of peace with the dactyls?" the ankylosaurus asked.

"I have started the conversation," she replied, "and I think that's quite enough. Yes, I'm neutral, but there is far too much history between both groups for me to have a valid opinion on what either of you should do. I believe you will have to work the matter out for yourselves, and I have high hopes for both sides."

"Teach us your system, then," Abnir said. "We will have to work and to think, and choices will be made about who should step forward to write with them first. All of this will take time. But you can tell them this: we will send someone. There are no promises here. But we will try."

"That's all I wanted," Cassidy said.

And so it went: she taught several humans and dinos, including Eshkar, Abnir, Belessunu, and the oviraptor of the council, how to communicate what she'd worked out with the dactyls so far. They gave her some bits of amber and resin-worked wood with some of their unusual technological touches to put in her backpack. Suggestions started for ways they might make the drawing process more efficient.

Cassidy spent the remainder of her time with them in minor games, discussions, and meals — bidding them farewell. Mashda returned her the following morning to the meeting spot, and found that the dactyls were watching for her well outside of the grove. Roc took her from there, and gave the corythosaurus a conspicuous amount of space until Cassidy was on her back. But it let the dino go, and proceeded to attempt to fly the little human itself. This time, there were dactyls at various angles and it made many stops, sharing vibrations with its colleagues.

"Good job!" Cassidy congratulated them. She was still on Roc's back, so there wasn't much more she could do, but she realized they were working on developing better techniques for carrying her. Oh, the chats she'd have with Gamgee when she got home!

Albatross was at the same flat drawing patch when Cassidy alighted, still sore and thoroughly thumped but better than before. "Hi, everyone!" she said with a wave.

None of them responded, of course.

Albatross began by drawing her backpack. She was shocked. "What, why?" She drew an arrow from the pack to a picture of herself. Albatross immediately jabbed the tip of its wing at the picture of the pack.

"Okay, okay," she said somewhat grumpily. She was truly excited about what studies might yield of the materials she'd collected. One item at a time, hoping to demonstrate that her stuff warranted respect, she laid out each item with care. She spaced them far apart, so that the dactyls would have no trouble getting close to them and would not disturb one thing while looking at another.

Her first aid kit, rations, and other gear that clearly

didn't come from here were examined with curiosity and at great length. But eventually they were returned to her. She saw with some annoyance that they were collecting the amber tech, resin-covered materials, and — while shooting her a dirty look — the smokes and an utuki plant she'd smuggled out of the tribe's belongings.

She knew that much, at least, would never get past either the tribespeople or the dactyls. What did surprise her was that they took everything that came from this world from her possessions. Even a fruit she'd been given purely as a snack, a bit of bark from one of the trees, and oviraptor feathers. Frustrated, she avidly pointed with the nearest stick at the picture of herself and the arrow, drawing more to emphasize: "That's mine!"

Albatross didn't waste effort on detail, drawing a simple down-open parabola for the Temple of Hearkening and a circle, somewhat above it, to indicate the portal she'd used. It then drew an utuki next to the circle, a double-headed arrow pointing at both the portal and the flower, and an X in the middle of the arrow's shaft.

They spent several hours going back and forth, refining their communication system even as they strove to work out the terms of an agreement. Cassidy inwardly accepted some time ago that they weren't going to let her take anything from this world on her return. What she was really struggling with — despite passing herself off as still arguing — was why they cared, why they were refusing *everything*. What did they care if she took tools and tech belonging to the dinos and humans that neither utuki nor dactyl could use or understand?

Ultimately, she concluded that this was partly the

price they were demanding of her. They weren't taking her to that cave in the sky without a cost to be paid. Which was fair. But everything from here? Yet she was allowed to keep the materials that she'd brought with her? Sighing, she conceded defeat. She couldn't risk dragging this out too long, as she was hoping they'd bring her back while she still had daylight.

They used a tight formation of not less than a dozen dactyls to get her above the canopy. Most of them were below or to the sides of Roc, who was carrying her again. Albatross had taken her effects, including the utuki, and left the circle of discussion with some ceremony. Cassidy couldn't hope to follow all of it. But it looked like they were taking care to have plenty of backup to catch her in case something went wrong.

Once free of the rainforest, she struggled to pull out her cell phone and get in some snapshots. It was like trying to take pics while on a canoe in the midst of rapids. Once they approached the portal, the flight slowed. From here, all she could see was the small span of a rocky cavern. Gamgee's team had made sure that she'd have to turn to go through the portal, because they didn't want anything or anyone who came looking to find them too easily.

Half of the group of dactyls flew around the portal every which way, clearly fearing and mistrusting it. Roc hesitated before getting close. Cassidy was profoundly disappointed that she hadn't gotten a chance to bring back anything from her exploration, but consoled herself that she'd learned a great deal. She'd be back.

Roc was trying different approaches.

"What's wrong?" Cassidy called out.

No response. Obviously.

Eventually, the dactyls around Roc and Cassidy gathered, facing the portal. They gave their friend some space. The human, being the person she was, looked down. Every time she did, it sent jolts of vertigo and joy through her gut and her spine. Roc's flight climbed a little, so that they were on par with the top borders of the portal. Its breaths came in the same way a human's does when bracing themselves.

As the dactyl brought her in for a landing, Cassidy shouted at the top of her lungs, "INCOMIIIING!"

"Don't shoot!" she added when she landed. "This is just my Über driver!"

ACKNOWLEDGEMENTS

The authors would like to pay special thanks to the *Slipstreamers* committee at Engen Books, including Amanda Labonté, Matthew LeDrew, AJ Ryan, Ellen Curtis, Erin Vance, and, Lauralana Dunne.

Without their tireless efforts, none of this would have been possible.

Special thanks to this episode's editor, Ali House.

Matthew Daniels would also like to thank Mandi Coates for a wonderful cover and his partner, Alisha, for being awesome and supportive. Also coffee and his three spazzy cats.

COMING SOON!
THE SECRET OF THE OHKS
BY JD RYOT & AJ RYAN!

The next incredible episode of Slipstreamers, *The Secret of the Ohks*, will be available soon, written with AJ Ryan!

While looking for a gem called The Lord Stone, Cassidy finds the world of Ohkshhon, a place of fantasy, magic, and medieval warriors! Caught in a war between the Ohks and elves, Cassidy must shield the prince from the machinations of a ghostwoman mage! Can she adapt to this mystical world in time to save the day?

ABOUT THE AUTHOR

Matthew Daniels is an author currently living in St. John's, Newfoundland.

He has over a dozen writing credits both locally and internationally, and his work had been featured in best-selling anthologies on five separate occasions. Stories include 'Grey Anatomy' in *Paragon*, 'Where With All' in *All Borders are Temporary*, and too many stories to count in the *From the Rock* series.

In December 2019 he was named a member of the Engen Books Board of Directors.

His first novel, *Diary of Knives*, was released in January 2021.

JD Ryot is the reclusive creator of the *Slipstreamers* series from Engen Books. JD is an avid fan of young adult literature and adventure serials. When asked if they had come to this world through a portal themselves, JD Ryot refused to answer. No record of their birth has ever been found... on this world.

www.ingramcontent.com/pod-product-compliance
Lightning Source LLC
Chambersburg PA
CBHW05201417O626
46808CB00007B/2922